I0718064

Broken Record

James C. Wolf

Broken Record
First edition, published 2018

Cover Artwork by Amy

Paperback ISBN-13: 978-1-942661-87-0

Published by Kitsap Publishing
P.O. Box 572
Poulsbo, WA 98370
www.KitsapPublishing.com

Printed in the United States of America

150-10 9 8 7 6 5 4 3 2 1

"We should be thankful we cannot see the horrors and degradations lying around our childhood, in cupboards and bookshelves, everywhere."

— Graham Greene

For Denise

PART ONE: BLACK PHANTOM

James C. Wolf

Detective Ron Steele
Cloverdale Police Dept
112 Broad St.
Cloverdale, CA 94525

RE: Our Discussion of Found Manuscript

Dear Det. Steele,

As we discussed enclosed is the manuscript recovered during our home remodel. Again, the workers said it was inside the wall behind a patch in the lath and plaster. The pages were not numbered. I numbered them in red ink before I realized what I was reading (sorry).

I don't know if it has any value, but after you've completed your investigation, if the manuscript is not considered evidence I would like to have it returned.

As always, I'm available to answer any questions you may have.

Sincerely,

Jennifer Haley

1

Henry J.
April 14, 1965

First off, let me say that I don't really see how this will change anything. Let me also say that I've never heard of a high school counselor being able to issue assignments. I know you said it's not an "assignment" and that it's voluntary but it still feels like homework and I get enough from my teachers, but I suspect you'll keep on about it until it's done. I also suspect that because you can write "Ph.D." after your name that you're not used to push back, and even with your repeated assurances of complete confidentiality, I'm filled with dread, with fear that this'll make things worse. I'll do it, but note that it's under protest.

I saw on the news this evening that it's been exactly one hundred years since President Lincoln was shot. I also saw that Richard Hickock and Perry Smith were hanged today for murdering that family in Kansas. Is there any meaning in that? I don't know.

I don't even know where to start; there are just too many beginnings and far too many endings. I suppose you could say that it started during the war. Not the war we're in now, even if Johnson doesn't call it war, or the war before in Korea. Maybe it started when my father got home from World War Two.

He shouldn't have even been in the war if you ask me. The draft age then was from eighteen to what? sixty-five? And if you were forty-five or younger then you were immediately liable to be drafted.

My mom said my father was thirty years old when his draft notice came. That was in June of 1943 and Mom was already two months pregnant with Tommy. My father had been a bookkeeper at the Ford dealership in Campbell California just trying to make sure that the debits equaled the credits then because the mailman had come he was spirited off to basic training to learn to kill Germans.

He'd been assigned to the 2nd Infantry Division. I still own a 2nd Infantry patch he wore, an Indian head in full headdress within a white star over a black shield. Despite spending hours in the library reading about the 2nd Infantry, I have no idea who designed the patch or what it's supposed to represent. My guess it was a holdover from a time when the U.S. Army was shootin' it's way across the country, one Indian after another all the way to here in California. Tommy gave me the patch.

The 2nd Infantry shipped out to Ireland that October of '43 and the following January Tommy was born while my father was preparing for the land invasion of Europe. His division landed on Omaha Beach on D-day plus 1--June 7, 1944, so he missed the slaughter of the early hours of the struggle. But he didn't miss the fight. Not by a long shot.

2nd Infantry Division took up the battle during the first week of June 1944 and they fought their way across Europe, arriving at Pilsen, Czechoslovakia when the Germans finally surrendered on May 8, 1945. All told the 2nd Infantry saw 305 days of combat. The division returned home to Fort Swift Texas on 22 July, as the Army would say, but my father wasn't with them. He'd been sent home and hospitalized on May 19th suffering from battle fatigue.

They don't even call it battle fatigue anymore. Now it's "Operational Exhaustion." Operational Exhaustion doesn't even sound like something that would happen to humans. It sounds like what happens when you rack up too many miles on your Chevy. Since battle fatigue no longer exists does that mean my father didn't have it? And even when it existed there weren't too many soldiers who served in World War Two who were diagnosed with battle fatigue. They had a tendency to get killed or wounded before any onset.

I read that symptoms of operational exhaustion begin to appear after about one hundred days of combat and that most soldiers will suffer its effects by two hundred days. My father saw three hundred and five days of combat. Three hundred and five days. And he wasn't some eighteen year-old with huge balls and no sense. He was thirty. He'd been armed with an adding machine and a half-dozen sharp pencils when the Army swapped them for an M-1 carbine and a bayonet.

After the army had spent him all up they pinned a Combat Infantry Badge on his pajamas and sent him home.

I don't know if he ever went back to work once he returned. As far back as my memory goes, he'd never worked. My earliest memories of my father are all much the same one to the next. They're like those "what's different in these two pictures" cartoons they have in the paper. My father sitting in his chair listening to the radio, sometimes wearing a different shirt, sometimes listening to the phonograph, sometimes with a plate of food resting on his lap, but almost always with a cigarette burning in his amber colored ashtray and his fingers worrying the musket right off that Combat Infantry Badge.

His ashtray sat on a footlocker my father kept next to his chair. The footlocker had been his during the war and it slept next to him like an old dog. I don't know what he kept in it. The first time I ever looked in the footlocker it was empty.

I have to say I'm surprised I was even born. Like most people it's hard to imagine their parents doing it, but my father could barely get a spoonful of soup up to his lips. How he got his...you know...up, I have no idea. I suspect my Mom just climbed on his lap in his chair one evening shortly after he got home, cigarette smoke curling up from the ashtray.

As a kid I had a Tonka dump truck that I employed to move and dump almost everything in the house. I'd play under my father's feet and fill the dump truck making whining, grinding heavy crane sounds while I lifted wooden blocks or books or National Geographic magazines with my crane arms and fill the bed of the dump truck. Once loaded to capacity I'd drive off making engine sounds, including several dozen gear shifts, to some other part of the house where I'd tilt the bed on its rear hinges and deposit my load. Then often, I'd reload the same items and drive them to someplace else in the house, many times to their original location, and dump them there. My father never told me to "play somewhere else" or to "clean up this mess" or to "pipe down." He just sat there listening to the radio over and around my loading and dumping, his cigarette smoldering in the ashtray.

Some people flick the ashes off their cigarettes like they're typing out War and Peace in Morse code. They'd puff then flick, flick, flick, flick then puff and tap, tap, tap, tap into an ashtray. Sometimes they'd roll the red embers on the tip around and around like they're shaping a worn out crayon. Puff, flick, tap, roll, Napoleon prepares to invade. Puff, flick, tap, roll, Anatol loses his leg. Puff, flick, tap, roll, Natasha smiles at Pierre. After several thousand flicks and taps the epilogue is a crushed cigarette butt. My father wasn't like that.

He smoked Lucky Strikes. By "smoked" I mean my father would light one, inhale, set it on the lip of the ashtray and let it burn away. Every couple of days he'd fill the ashtray. My Mom would have me empty it, which was one of my favorite things. I'd pour the butts and ashes into the bed of the dump truck and wheel it off to the trash. I couldn't count the hours I worked as a dump truck operator... if only I had been on the clock.

It was during summer vacation 1952 when the

picture changed. That was between kindergarten and first grade. I'd awakened and worked my way down from the top bunk. Tommy used to sleep on the top bunk until one night when he fell out of bed; from then on I had the top. I liked it fine but it did get hot up there in summer. I slept in just my underpants because even the thought of wearing pajamas made me sweat.

I came downstairs in my white drawers and saw that my father's chair was empty. He wasn't in the bathroom. There was no cigarette burning itself out in the ashtray. Then I saw the Combat Infantry Badge on the armrest of my father's chair. I could never remember not seeing it in his hand. The silver musket floating on a light blue bar was worn smooth, as were the leaves of the oak wreath that shrouded the bar. I didn't touch it. I just looked and something told me the picture would never be the same.

My father had left. No discussion. No emotional fight. No tearful goodbyes or lies about going out for a newspaper. He was just gone. Still is. And the funny thing is nothing much changed after he was gone; at least not then.

It's getting late and I think that's enough for now.

2

Maybe it didn't start with World War Two. Maybe that was an ending and it started with my father's departure. Maybe it started with Tommy's Schwinn bicycle. Actually it couldn't have started there, it would have to have started before that.

A few days after my father left, Mom sent Tommy and me to her parents' home up in Los Altos. Tommy put up a fuss because he'd been playing ball in the Junior Hardball League and he'd have to quit the team. But Mom stuck to her guns saying that she didn't want to worry about us during vacation. Funny thing is, it wasn't like we were doing anything different when my father was home. It wasn't like he was watching us or making lunch or anything. Even before he left, during summers it was always Tommy who'd watch over me, Tommy making lunch, Tommy putting Mercurochrome and bandages over my scraped knees. Despite my father sitting there in his chair, it was really Tommy who was the man of the house. But maybe Mom worried about how it would look, so off we went.

Being sent to her parents' also gave Grandpa cheap labor for the summer. That was okay; "cheap" actually meant cheap, not free, and Tommy and I, well we needed the money.

Even though we lived pretty close to Mom's parents, until then we hadn't spent much time visiting. We'd go up for Christmas (usually a few days before the 25th) and sometimes on Easter, but that was about it. My father never went with us. Tommy said our grandparents visited our house once but Grandpa just yelled at our father until Mom asked them to leave. According to Tommy, Grandpa didn't think it was manly to allow a woman to be the breadwinner. I suppose I was there when this happened, but I surely don't remember it.

Grandma and Grandpa lived in a small house on a large parcel of land. Their house was a white stucco two-bedroom with dark green trim and a red-clay tile roof. There were three lawns bordering the house that my grandparents called the "north lawn," "south lawn" and "east lawn." There was no "west lawn." Each of the three lawns was fully enclosed by foliage, except one stretch of the north lawn, which was open on the side facing the house. And each of the three lawns featured similar stone sculptures. On the north lawn sat a sculpture of three women draped in robes standing arm to arm and back to back forming a circle. Resting on the east lawn was a sundial held up by three similar, but differently adorned women. In the center of the south lawn was a fishpond with a fountain gracing the middle of the pond. Again, the fountain had three similarly robed women. Grandma said they represented the nine muses of Greek Mythology.

The driveway made up part of the north border where it ended in a square building comprised of a garage, Grandpa's workshop and a pool house. On one wall of the pool house there had to be at least a hundred abalone shells that Grandpa had nailed in place over the years. It shone like a sparkling rainbow. Just beyond the pool house was a rectangular concrete aboveground pool that was about five feet deep and dry. I'd never seen water in it except the occasional rainwater. Grandma's flower garden took up the southeast corner and led to a brick barbeque and a vine-covered arbor. The west side of the lot was a small orchard of fruit, nut and citrus trees. Concrete sidewalks meandered around the house, skirting the lawns and winding through the garden.

At first Grandpa put us to work harvesting walnuts, almonds, lemons, apricots and cumquats. This we did for ten cents an hour each. I didn't mind the work except for two things: one, Grandma made us wear her old straw hats to keep us from getting sunburned, but they were too big and mine kept sliding down over my eyes (and I'm not even mentioning the pink gingham hat band) and two, Grandpa gave both Tommy and me identical buckets then proceeded to criticize me because Tommy could gather more fruit or nuts. I've never been all that competitive, and criticism surely wasn't going to change that. All it did was make me gather less; part out of anger and part because I had time to think and thinking about it, it wasn't to my advantage to work faster--we weren't being paid by the bushel, we were paid by the hour.

So Grandpa kept up his critique and I kept up my work slowdown. It had become a battle of wills for several days until Tommy started putting some of his harvest in my bucket. He balanced the buckets out saying, "This'll shut him up." Tommy was right. Once Tommy started doing that, Grandpa's critique didn't shift to praise, it just ceased, which was all I wanted, so then I resumed working at my normal speed and peace was restored.

After the harvest, Grandma had us weed her

flower garden. I enjoyed crawling around in the dirt, pulling out weeds by the roots and cleaning up the flowerbed. I liked how I could immediately see the results of my work. Grandma would come out and watch over us, maybe to supervise but mostly to teach. She'd talk about fertilizer (her preference was chicken manure) and perennials and which flowers came from bulbs and how to prune roses. I liked it although I don't remember half of what she told us. Tommy, well, Tommy was bored; he wanted more activity. We satisfied that desire at the end of the workday.

In the garage, Grandpa had a gold-painted pedal car that I think dated to before the war. Tommy said he used to drive it around but by then he was too big to fit his legs inside. I could barely fit myself and pedaling was an ordeal. But what we did...one of us would sit our butt down on the seat with our legs outside the car resting on the fenders next to the hood with the steering wheel between our knees. Then the other would push the car around the sidewalks and driveway and sometimes out onto the street. We'd do that for hours. I got the best of it; Tommy was faster and had more stamina. Tommy didn't complain that I'd run out of gas sooner than he'd like, but when I'd push it was to continual chorus of "Faster!"

Grandpa drove a 1950 Aqua Green Studebaker Champion with the optional "Hill Holder" clutch. It had the chrome (Grandpa called it chromium) bullet nose that had become Studebaker's signature. Grandpa had upgraded to the leather seats over the standard cloth and I remember that even after a few years the back seat still smelled like new shoes.

I was pushing Tommy out on the street barely running on fumes when Grandpa pulled the Champion into the driveway. Tommy steered us behind him. Grandpa got out of his car saying "I've got something for you two." Tommy and I looked at each other sharing a single thought, "I wonder what?"

Keys jingled as Grandpa flipped through them on his key ring. He must have had thirty keys on the ring and he jingle-jangled through several before striking gold. The Champion had two keys, one for the door and ignition and another for the glove compartment and trunk. The trunk was operated with a lock and handle that formed the right wing of the chrome (chromium) Studebaker emblem. Grandpa used his left hand to turn the key and his right to lift the handle. I don't know if they had to be done simultaneously but that's how he always did it. The first thing I saw was the spare tire in its cradle on the right side of the trunk standing upright like it was at attention. Next to the spare tire were nine one-gallon cans of paint--seven white and two green.

Paint. He got us paint. I remember thinking

"paint?" just as Tommy said it aloud. Grandpa pointed out it wasn't just paint, it was house-paint: Sherwin-Williams Outside Paint in Gloss White and Sagamore Green. He had us each grab a gallon while he grabbed two and follow him to his workshop. He was saying something about all little boys liking to paint and Tom Sawyer whitewashing a fence. Tommy said Tom Sawyer got other kids to whitewash the fence. I guess Tommy realized what was in store for us and that in this case Grandpa was Tom Sawyer.

Grandpa's workshop was made from sawdust. At least that's how it seemed since a fine layer covered every surface and tool. He had a table saw, a band saw, a whole collection of different hand saws mounted on nails on the wall, dozens of hand tools, paintbrushes and rollers also mounted on nails, shelves laden with glass jars full of nuts and bolts and nails and washers and upholstery tacks and stuff I didn't recognize, piles of various lengths of wood, several ladders and an assortment of either odds or ends. He had a metal stool with a cracked blue leather seat. On his workbench he'd mounted three sizes of vises (the only tool I was allowed to operate) and a drill press. The band saw, table saw and drill press were all Craftsman and were probably ordered through the Sears Roebuck catalog. We stacked the paint on the workbench then Tommy and I went out for the rest of the cans;

it took us two trips (Tommy carried two gallons on the final trip). While we brought the rest of the paint, Grandpa selected several brushes, rollers, paint trays and paint-covered coffee cans and had also placed them on the workbench. Grandpa said we'd start early the next morning.

I was assigned trim duty. After breakfast Grandpa led Tommy and me outside where he had laid out brushes and rollers and paint cans. He poured some of the Sagamore Green trim paint into a squat one-pound MJB coffee can, gave me a brush and set me to painting the window trim. Tommy got a quick lesson in rolling on paint then was turned loose on the wall. Grandpa checked my work and told me not to worry about getting paint on the glass; he'd clean it up later with a scraper. Grandpa left us saying to come get him when we needed more paint.

Once I finished painting all the trim I could reach from the ground, Tommy helped me set up a ladder. Tommy refilled my MJB can rather than bothering Grandpa. The sun came out and warmed the day. Tommy shirked off his shirt. While rolling, Tommy asked what I was going to do with my money. I hadn't really thought about it, and I told him so. "How much do you suppose we'll earn?" I asked. Tommy said he wasn't quite sure since we'd just started painting, but he'd added up the hours we'd worked 'til then and figured we were closing in on two dollars each. I didn't know how much two dollars could buy then, still don't, but truth be told it didn't sound like much. I asked Tommy what you could get for two dollars. He said to tell him what I wanted and he'd tell me if it costs more than two dollars. "How about a Radio Flyer wagon?" I asked. Tommy said nope, that I couldn't even get half a wagon. "What about M&M's?" I asked. "Sure. A lot of them," Tommy said. I asked if I could get enough to fill the coffee can I was painting with. Tommy was pretty sure I could. I asked if I could buy a Ronson Electric Shaver, but Tommy just wanted to know what I was going to do with that. I didn't know and I told him so, it had just popped into my head. Tommy said no I couldn't get an electric shaver. He went on to say that we couldn't get much apiece, but if we combined our money, then it might be worth something. Looking back on it I suspect he'd been thinking that all along.

We didn't paint the next morning. It was Sunday. Grandma had gone to the Goodwill to get suits for church for Tommy and me because "since we were sprouting like weeds in a summer rain it didn't make sense to buy new from the Sears Roebuck." She'd found a powder blue suit coat with some type of crest on the breast pocket and matching short pants for me, and a navy blue sport coat and contrasting charcoal grey slacks

for Tommy. I had to wear a belt to hold the short
pants up; I didn't want to wear either. Grandma
combined the suits with white dress shirts and
matching red clip-on bow ties. She said she wasn't
about to make us wear someone else's old shoes so
we wore our PF Flyers.

Grandma splashed some of Grandpa's Lucky
Tiger hair tonic on our heads, parted our hair with a
small black comb and slicked it down good. Suits
and slicked down hair, I guess after two thousand
years God decided flowing hair and robes weren't
good enough anymore.

Grandma and Grandpa loaded us up into the car
and drove us to church. It wasn't a Catholic church,
which I'd been to once (I liked all the standing and
kneeling); it was some type of Protestant church.
We were a bit late and the faithful were all moving
in through two huge doors. We hustled out of the
car but had to wait just outside the doors while
someone said the Invocation. After the "amens"
we whisked in. The congregation stood and sang
in measured voices. I could make out the word
"cheerful" in the song but the solemn voices seemed
anything but cheerful. On the wall a wooden
plaque displayed the numbers for hymns; I grabbed
a hymnal. I could read a little bit, but I already
knew my numbers. Number 595, Now to the King
of something I couldn't make out, 1851. Number
43, something Is something something (the only

word I knew was 'Is'), 1923. Number 186, The
Old something Cross, 1913. Number 204, Rock
of Ages, no date. There were two more but by then
Grandma took the hymnal away.

We sat when the singing stopped. The pews were
dark stained hardwood, solid as stone. Some
man was then at the lectern reading very stern
announcements. My feet hung off the end of the
pew as I sat all the way back, when I knocked my
sneakers together dust shook loose and drifted to
the floor. Tommy whispered to knock it off. A dour
man rose and launched into an unhappy sermon
about the good news.

I thought about the difference in Gods. The
Catholic God was Latin and He liked His followers
active; standing, sitting, kneeling over and over.
This God liked quiet believers, who sat still and
sang dutifully, purposefully and shunned joy. I
don't know about the messages from either God,
neither one I understood, but I liked the Catholic
one better; the standing and kneeling made time
move faster.

The monotony was broken when it was time for
the Eucharist. Men in dark suits broke bread into
small pieces and placed them on amber serving
trays while the minister or pastor (I didn't know
which he used) prayed over the Body of Christ.
Then the suits served the congregation pew-by-pew.
When the tray came down our pew I noticed while

I took a piece of bread that the trays were the same color as my father's ashtray. I popped the bread in my mouth. I think it was Wonderbread.

"Oh no," I whispered.

"What?" Tommy whispered back.

"I got some of Jesus on my shirt."

"Don't wipe it off."

"Why not?" I asked.

"Because," he whispered, "you're not supposed to let Jesus touch the ground."

"I thought that was the flag."

"You two hush," Grandma hissed.

I brushed the crumbs on the pew to keep them from hitting the floor when I stood.

It took the better part of two weeks to paint the house. The best part was painting the trim along the roofline. Grandpa leaned the extension ladder against the tiled roof and Tommy and I scrambled up. I got on the roof itself while Tommy stood on the ladder. Grandpa handed a bucket of paint up to Tommy who set it on the roof between us. Then we both painted the trim, me laying on the roof about three feet from the bucket with my head over the edge. I painted upside down as Tommy painted through and around the ladder. We inch-wormed around the roofline talking and sweating and painting until we finally met up to where we started. I remember the sun on my back and the heat radiating from the roof, it felt like a soft embrace. I don't recall all that Tommy and I talked about, but it doesn't matter really; it doesn't diminish the memory of that time, of that summer, spending time with my big brother just working and talking. It feels like a magical dream.

We were on the last stretch of roof trim when we heard the mailman coming up the walk. He carried a large box and Grandpa came out of the house before the mailman got to the door. Grandpa looked like a grin with legs. "What do you think that is?" I asked Tommy. He said he didn't know but whatever it was it didn't look like it was too heavy. We finished the roof trim trying to divine what was in the box. We were wrong on every guess.

After finishing the trim we washed up in a big stone sink in the back porch, sharing a bar of Palmolive soap. I washed off as much as I could, but I wouldn't be surprised to find that after all these years I still had some dark Sagamore Green paint hiding somewhere on my body. We dried ourselves (mostly) and bounded into the house to find out what was in the box.

The kitchen was empty, as was the dining room. We found our grandparents in the living room, the box opened before them on their circular coffee table. I noted that the box had been wrapped in plain brown paper and was hand lettered with a return address from some company called O'Neill's. Grandpa pulled from the box what looked to me like a black Buck Rogers space suit. Tommy must have been thinking along the same lines because he asked, "Is that for outer space?" "Under water," Grandpa responded. Grandpa explained that Grandma wouldn't go diving with him anymore. Grandma said the water was "just too darned cold." But, Grandpa said, these new diving suits were made of neoprene foam rubber and were supposed to keep them warm. "Warm 'er'," Grandma corrected. I asked when they were going to try them out. "Tomorrow."

The sun hadn't had its first cup of coffee when we were on the road the next morning. Tommy and I knelt on the Studebaker's leather bench seat and stared out the back window watching the sun rise as Grandpa headed west on San Antonio Road. After passing the Los Altos town center, Grandpa turned south. I didn't exactly catch the name of the street as it faded in the distance but I think it was Foothill Boulevard. We followed the boulevard to a small community called Monte Vista. Grandpa steered the Champion left on to Stevens Creek Boulevard. Just after turning, Stevens Creek Boulevard heads down and up a narrow valley. Grandpa gunned the Studebaker down the valley so he'd have enough momentum to make it up the other side. For two young boys in the back seat, it was a blast. Tommy named that stretch of road "the fun hill" and whenever we subsequently spoke of it that's what we called it. About a mile and a half after the fun hill, Grandpa hung a right. We drove for several miles when Tommy spotted the first sign calling the road Highway 9. Highway 9 bent around the southwest foothills of Saratoga.

We finally came to a junction in Saratoga where Highway 9 split in two. The right branch led towards Big Basin winding around and over the Coast Ranges in a series of risky hairpin turns and treacherously narrow cliff edge stretches, passing through Boulder Creek and Ben Lomond, before spilling into Santa Cruz as River Road. The left branch of Highway 9 connected Saratoga with Los Gatos where it joined Highway 17. Grandma lobbied for the right branch, which was more scenic and had been the old way to get to the coast until 17 was opened in 1940. Grandpa countered with "17 is faster" and would be easier on the engine, so that was that.

Grandpa was unaware that we'd run into stop and go traffic just outside of Los Gatos because of construction on the new Lexington Reservoir. But once we were passed that it was open road.

The smooth highway angled up through the hills and Grandpa turned his attention to the engine's heat indicator as the Studebaker's six cylinder motor strained to maintain speed. I watched over Grandpa's shoulder as the gauge register crept out of the normal range and closer to the "H". Grandpa downshifted to second to crest the ridge and sped downhill, the temperature gauge falling, matching our descent. This process became a pattern-- temperature rising, speed dropping, summit, speed increasing, temperature decreasing--before we finally rolled down into Santa Cruz.

Instead of following Ocean Street down to the shore, Grandpa turned north on Highway 1. We continued out of Santa Cruz and north past Natural Bridges State Beach. A short time later Grandpa turned left off the highway. The road traversed some railroad tracks where it gave way from asphalt to dry compacted dirt. Less than a half a mile down the dirt road, Grandpa pulled to a stop and shut off the engine. "Where are we?" Tommy asked. Grandpa told him it was private property. Grandpa knew the owner and they had an agreement that Grandpa could dive there if he'd share his catch. I think he said something more, but by then I was out of the car.

I remember filling my lungs with the cool salt air. I toed the heel of my shoes to slip them off, followed by my socks. I scuffed around on the parched dirt creating miniature dust storms. While Grandpa unlocked the Champion's trunk I rolled up the cuffs of my pants. Grandpa lifted the two wetsuits from the shipping box, laying them out on the hood of the car. He went back to the trunk for a can of talc and a box of cornstarch. "What's that for?" I asked. He said that the powder would make it easier to put the suits on and would help minimize tearing. I asked if he had to mix them, but Grandpa explained that they just recommend the talc but he didn't have enough and figured cornstarch would work just as well and it was less expensive.

From the trunk Grandma handed out two red scotch plaid thermos jugs, one each for Tommy and me. She then gave us a brown wicker picnic basket and told us to follow a small trail down to the water; she and Grandpa would be along in short order.

Tommy led the way through the narrow trail encroached by tall dried grass and brush. "Stay away from that," he said pointing to a bush with slick shiny leaves. He explained that it was poison oak and would make you swell up and itch like crazy. "How do you know?" I asked. Tommy said a kid in school had it, even on his nuts, so his teacher showed the class pictures of poison oak, poison ivy and another one that he couldn't remember. "How'd it get on his nuts?" I asked. "I don't know," he said, "but to be safe don't touch it and keep your nuts in your pants." That made me laugh.

The trail gave way to a small cove where a sandy beach was embraced by big rocks and boulders. I ran down to the wet sand and tried to see how close I could get to the water without getting wet. Tommy sat on the sand and took off his shoes and socks. He came up beside me as I backed away from the last reach of a wave. Tommy realized I was trying to keep my feet dry so he picked me up and carried me down the shore and held me over the water. I lifted my feet while pleading for him to stop. But the more I lifted my feet the more he'd lower me. Finally I could no longer hold up my feet, so I slammed them down in the water and sent a splash on Tommy's pants. Then I took out running. He had me in seconds and was about to drop me in the surf when we spied Grandma and Grandpa coming down the trail. They looked like they'd been dipped in licorice. They were dripping in black except their bare hands and heads, and their feet shod in old basketball shoes. Grandpa carried a burlap sack that clanked as he walked. Grandma toted some towels and a large blanket.

   From the burlap sack Grandpa removed two straight iron bars and two lengths of metal with both ends bent at ninety degrees about six or seven inches apart. All four had holes drilled in them that had been laced with thin strips of leather. He also removed two D-ring canvas belts while Grandma laid out the blanket. Grandpa threaded the canvas belt through the leather lace of one of the tools and was affixing the belt around his waist when I asked, "What're those for?" He said the straight ones were for prying abalone from the rocks and the bent one to measure to make sure they were mature enough to take. Looking back on it, I'm not sure how much of that I completely understood, but after watching the tools in use I got it. Grandpa had Grandma tie one of the pry bars to his right wrist then he did the same for her. Grandma wrapped the other belt and measuring tool around her waist as she followed Grandpa to a wave-tossed outcropping of rocks. Tommy and I trailed behind them.

Black-shelled mussels covered the sides of the rocks and the tops were crowned by deep green seaweed. The seaweed swayed with the advancing and receding waves like Baptists in a revival meeting. Sidestepping tide pools, Tommy and I scaled the slippery rocks up to the bare dry surfaces the waves couldn't reach.

"In the shallows," Grandpa said, "you can see the abalone, but in the deeper water you have to feel for them. There's one there." Grandpa pointed to a bulge in a crevasse between two rocks. "I don't see it," Tommy said. I did. It looked like a wart growing on the face of the rock. I pointed it out to Tommy. "Where?" he said. I tried to describe it but for some reason he just couldn't see it. It made me think of those "find the hidden object" pictures where at first glance it was just a simple landscape but when you looked closer you could see things like a pair of scissors or a troll or a bucket. Tommy just couldn't see the bucket.

Grandpa pried the abalone from the rock and showed it to Tommy. Tommy said, "Oh I see where it was now," but I suspect he was lying.

I was assigned to help Grandma find abalone in the shallows, while Tommy helped Grandpa. I found two right off. Grandpa found one on his own. He took that one and the two Grandma got and put them in the burlap sack. Tommy still couldn't find any abalone so eventually he just found a dry rock to lie on while he held onto the burlap sack letting it soak in the sea. I liked fishing for abalone and for several years afterward it had become an annual event for Grandpa and me. This was Tommy's only time.

We harvested about eight or nine abalone before calling it quits. Tommy and I laid out on the blanket to dry where I promptly fell asleep. When I awoke, Grandma and Grandpa had changed and Grandma was digging sandwiches from the picnic basket. After eating we packed up and headed out.

Grandpa stopped at the landowners gray weathered house and dropped off a couple of abalone. Per Grandma's wish we drove home over highway 9, the Studebaker's hard tires singing out around the dangerous hairpin curves. Funny, but even though it was a greater distance, it seemed like it took half the time to get home as it did to drive to the coast. The goings always seem longer than the comings. I'm not sure why that is.

I watched as Grandpa cleaned the abalone, cut them into steaks and pounded them out to tenderize them. We dined that night on fresh abalone. That was the last night of our stay; Mom was coming in the morning to fetch us. After dinner Grandpa sat at his desk and tallied up our work hours on a green-lined ledger book. We'd earned nine dollars and eighty cents each. Grandma had him round it up and Grandpa handed us two ten-dollar bills.

3

The Black Phantom was a beauty. Swatches of red highlighted the gloss black paint that gave it the illusion of speed. The chrome trim and fenders made it sparkle like treasure. "Schwinn" in gold script outlined in red adorned the tank and on the chain guard read the name "Black Phantom" in black and gold. It had a lever pull front brake and a black luggage rack that held a blazing red taillight.

We'd pooled our money, just as Tommy had wanted, and bought the used Phantom from a teenager down the street. The teenager had upgraded to a 1939 Ford Coupe, the Schwinn thus relegated to a corner in their garage. We bought the bicycle with part of the money and used the rest for parts and paint to restore it. The bike had seen a few accidents and had nasty scratches on the fork, right pedal and the back part of the frame. The right hand grip was missing a large chunk. But the rest of the bike was spared, including the brown leather seat and the whitewall tires.

Tommy also bought a can of Testors red enamel paint for me. Here was the deal: we'd go in together to buy the Schwinn and Tommy would repaint his old Western Flyer and give it to me. As part of the deal he'd teach me to ride. In addition, he'd let me help him work on the bikes. The final caveat I threw in was he had to paint the Western Flyer first.

School had started back up by then and Tommy and I would usually walk if we got up early enough. We went to the San Tomas School, me in first grade, Tommy in fourth. If we were late or it was raining Mom would give us a ride on her way to the Farmer's Union Packing House on Orchard City Drive.

Mom wanted us to paint the bikes down in the basement but that's not what we did. When we descended to the basement we found that Mom had wrestled my father's chair down there. It sat there by the furnace with his footlocker and ashtray placed neatly next to it. I could almost see him sitting in the chair, dust from the basement swirling around it in mock cigarette smoke. It was eerie. I think Tommy felt the same way, but he didn't say anything. He turned back to the stairs and I followed him up. He told Mom there was too much dust in the basement to paint so they agreed we'd paint in the back yard.

For some reason Tommy decided we would disassemble the bikes up in our room. I'm sure I knew then why he wanted to do it that way, but for the life of me, I can't seem to remember now. But whatever the reason, we thumped and bumped the bikes upstairs and into our room where Tommy had laid out flattened corrugated cardboard boxes to protect the floor. We started on the Western Flyer. Tommy handed me a crescent wrench and showed me which nuts to remove. If they were on too tight, Tommy would break them loose then have me finish taking them off. Some parts required a screwdriver and others needed pliers to keep the entire bolt from turning. We dismantled the entire bicycle except the pedal assembly using just a flat-tipped screwdriver, a pair of slip-joint pliers and a crescent wrench. The pedal assembly we left untouched. Tommy put the small parts inside the Aladdin Hy-Lo lunch box he sometimes carried to school.

We moved the flattened cardboard to the back yard then brought down the bike frame, fenders and forks for painting. Tommy wrapped the pedals and sprocket with newspaper and taped it down using masking tape. Then we took turns shaking the can of spray paint to insure it was well mixed, then Tommy took to painting the Flyer. I wanted to try but Tommy was worried about getting runs in the finish so I stood by and received a light dusting of Testors Red to go with the Sagamore Green trim paint I already wore. We had to let it set for several hours before it was dry enough to touch.

Tommy jury-rigged training wheels onto the Western Flyer as part of the reassembly process. The trainers had footpads built into them to allow Tommy to ride on back if he wanted. He didn't use them.

When he first got the bike down to the street, it wouldn't go at all. Tommy had attached the training wheels in such a way that the back tire didn't touch the road surface and would just spin freely as I pedaled. We flipped the bike over and Tommy raised the training wheels just a notch. I was then able to ride but didn't have to think about balancing the Flyer.

After awhile I became proficient at pedaling, steering and braking so Tommy raised the training wheels a couple of more notches so that I had to concentrate on balancing. Tommy told me that if I felt like I was losing balance, just lean the bike to one side and the training wheels would keep me upright. That's what I did.

Once I could ride without having to lean the bike

for balance Tommy took the left side training wheel completely off. He reminded me to lean to the right if I thought I was losing my balance. I rode around for about fifteen minutes, never once needing to lean right at which time Tommy took the training wheels off altogether. Tommy taught me to ride all in the course of one afternoon.

The following Friday I was riding on the street out in front of the house when Bob pulled to a stop at the curb. In my mind it's always pronounced "Baawwb." Mom had only been home for a few minutes and was preparing dinner. Tommy was upstairs carefully applying masking tape on the Black Phantom over the parts he didn't want painted. I'd helped him take the bike apart, but grew bored with the masking. I saw Tommy's face in the upstairs window when Bob set the parking brake on his heather green '48 Chrysler Windsor convertible. I rode close to look at the chrome spoke wheels and whitewall tires. Bob told me, "Don't get too close, kid."

Bob wasn't as tall as my father but probably outweighed him by forty pounds. His dark wavy hair was slicked straight back and held in place by some hair treatment. Bob climbed out of the car, straightened his beige slacks and tightened his orange tie. I noticed he'd left his plaid sport coat, a maroon, gray, beige and black slubby wool job, resting over the passenger seat.

Mom met Bob at the door and said she'd "be just a minute." Mom had straightened her updo and was wearing lipstick. She had changed her dress. She waved me over and introduced me to Bob. Bob put a heavy paw on my head (I got a whiff of the distinct smell of Vitalis) and rubbed saying "Hey there, kid." I don't think I said anything. Tommy pushed past Mom and in a voice deeper than normal asked Bob what he wanted. Bob looked at Mom who said that Bob was a new co-worker and was taking her to see a picture. "High Noon," Bob said. Tommy and I hadn't yet seen High Noon and I gave him a look that said, "say something," but he didn't. Somehow I believed then that if we didn't see it that night we'd never get a chance to see it. Bob was taking Mom and he was also taking away our chance to see the movie. I didn't understand about the length of a movie run and since we didn't own a TV, I hadn't considered television let alone late night reruns. I never did see the film.

We left Bob on the stoop while Mom took us to the kitchen, giving Tommy instructions as we walked. "Dinner is on plates in the oven. I already did most of the dishes so you and Henry just need to wash and dry your plates and silverware. No radio after seven. Lock the door and leave the porch light on and you two in bed by eight." Tommy mumbled something that I didn't catch and Mom was out the door.

Tommy was upset and didn't eat much of his dinner. I didn't know then why he was bothered so much, but looking back on it, he'd been the man of the house for so long that he couldn't help but regard Bob as a potential interloper. He wouldn't have known the word "interloper" (and neither would I) but he'd have known how it felt.

Tommy scraped most of his dinner into the garbage. He ran the hot water in the sink and washed our dinner dishes, handing them to me to dry.

We didn't listen to the radio; Tommy wasn't in the mood. We went upstairs where Tommy resumed masking the Black Phantom. It was slow going when Tommy started masking over the pin striping. He cut several thin strips of tape and pressed them down. He used a paring knife from the kitchen to get them just right. But he didn't get much accomplished and I could tell something was bothering him. "What's wrong?" I asked. Tommy said he just didn't like that guy is all and he didn't know what Mom was doing going with him to movies and she should be here with us and she should have gone with us instead. Then he sat quietly for several minutes. Finally he looked at the alarm clock and told me to get ready for bed. He never mentioned the fact that Mom was still married to our father.

Tommy didn't get in bed. After he turned the

lights out he stood by the window watching the street below and listening.

I awoke to the squeak of brakes and the ratcheting grind of a parking brake being engaged. Tommy was still at the window. I asked him what time it was. "A little before ten," he said. "Is that them?" I asked. It was, so I crawled to the foot of my bed where I was able to look out the window to the street. I heard the "chunk" of a car door closing before I could see and was able to spot Mom halfway up the walk. Bob was in the process of getting out of the car to walk Mom to the door. He stopped when he was just at the back of the car. Mom said something I didn't catch, but Bob said, "Okay then. I'll see you at work." There was an exchange of "goodnights" and Bob drove off as Mom was still keying the lock. Tommy climbed in bed as I slipped under my quilt. I asked Tommy if he thought Bob would come back. "Go to sleep," he said.

Bob did come back. Two days later they went out for Sunday dinner. Tommy had complained that we should be allowed to go with them. Mom said that Bob had suggested the same thing but she didn't think it was a good idea and it was final and she wasn't discussing it any further. Tommy pouted upstairs while I helped Mom make our dinner. She boiled some elbow noodles then oversaw me as I cut some cheddar cheese into chunks.

She strained the noodles, dropped the chunks of cheese in then used some milk and cornstarch to makes a sauce. She had me open a can of cream of mushroom soup and some tuna fish, reminding me to drain the oil from the fish. She scooped both into the noodles and mixed it all together. Then she poured it into a casserole dish and sprinkled some breadcrumbs over it. She told me to go upstairs and tell Tommy that when we where ready to eat, to turn the oven on for 15 minutes and to be careful getting the casserole out.

Tommy just sat on his bed as I repeated Mom's instructions. Then he looked at me and said, "We're ready to paint the black."

Together we transported the Schwinn's frame out to the backyard, taking care not to tear the tape and newspaper he'd used to mask it. Tommy sent me back upstairs to fetch the Phantom's forks while he prepared the bike for painting. When I got back I saw that Tommy had set the bottom of the frame on a shoe box and had run the broom, bristled end up, through the neck. The handle of the broom was buried a few inches in the dirt, but it held the bike firm. Tommy expertly applied the paint in long even strokes, getting just a little overspray on the broom. When the paint became tacky he sprayed a second coat.

The second coat was almost dry to the touch when Bob arrived. He wore the same wool sport coat, but this time over gray slacks, a light gray button-down and a maroon and gold striped tie.

Mom was out of the house when we got 'round front and Bob opened the car door for her. She closed it herself. She waggled her fingers at Tommy and me and mouthed "toodle-oo." Bob pulled away from the curb. Tommy sat down on the porch, elbows on knees, chin on hands. I sat next to him and mimicked his position.

After sitting there awhile, Tommy rose and went inside, me at his heels. He turned the oven on and checked the clock. "C'mon," he said and I followed him out back. We gathered up the dry frame of the Black Phantom and carried it upstairs. Tommy told me to take the tape and paper off, being careful to pull the tape back on itself so it won't peel off any of the fresh paint. I felt both the honor and responsibility of this task. If I messed it up Tommy would have to redo it all. Tommy brought the forks up and watched as I finished removing all of the masking. He approved my work. "Now what?" I asked. "Dinner," he said.

Tommy used Mom's oven mitts to slide the casserole dish from the hot oven. He scooped out two servings of macaroni and cheese into cereal bowls and we sat down to eat. We weren't half finished when we heard a car door slam and the chirp of tires peeling out. Tommy got to the kitchen window in time to see Bob's taillights. "Mom's home already," he said. Mom stormed through the front door slamming it behind her. Now both Tommy and I were in the doorway to the kitchen. Mom was muttering under her breath. She looked up at us then continued upstairs, shutting the bedroom door behind her. Tommy and I returned in silence to our meal.

"That was a mistake," Mom said after she had come downstairs and saw we had finished eating and had washed our bowls. She got the left over macaroni and cheese from the fridge, dished out a plate and began eating it...cold.

We never asked what happened.

Late that night I awoke with a sense that something was wrong. Tommy was at the window looking out. "What is it?" I asked. He said he thought Bob was out there. "That's his car, right?" he said. I looked out the window and saw the heather green Chrysler across the street and several houses down. It was the first time I saw it with the top up, but it was Bob all right.

We watched a long time when I noticed smoke had started billowing from the tailpipe. "He started the car," I said. The Chrysler left the curb and slowly drove past, the headlights off.

This "assignment" is ridiculous. I'm sitting here scratching down word after miserable word and it won't change a thing. Every word is a bee sting, every sentence cuts, every paragraph becomes infected with green pus that won't heal. How is this supposed to make anything better? Looking back is like seeing the long row of dominoes, one having crashed down on the other again and again crushing our hopes and dreams and lives. It doesn't matter where it started or how it started, because each domino was already firmly in place and the hand of fate, or God, or whatever deemed it time to nudge the first in line.

The truth doesn't set anyone free, it's just another

brick loaded onto the burdens we all carry. I stopped diving for abalone with my grandfather because I learned the truth about the kind of man he could be. Am I better off, a better person, because I learned the truth? I don't know. I loved diving with him. And when he died and left me his wetsuits, well just like my memories of him, I boxed them up and buried them. They were fine there simply gathering dust until you felt that somehow writing this down would bring me some kind of clarity or acceptance or peace. It's just making things worse.

I'm not sure it matters much that you said this will help in the long run or that you'll make sure that the time I've spent (wasted) on this won't affect my final grades. I'm an eighteen year-old male on the cusp of graduating from high school. As I see it my future holds the possibility of bleeding out from a head wound in a jungle in Southeast Asia, or bleeding out from a head wound while protesting what is obviously a war we can't win (Jesus did we learn nothing from Korea or the French?) or bleeding out my soul from a thousand head wounds trying to fit into a society I'm not sure I believe in. We've distorted the ideals of "all for one and one for all" to just "all for one, period." So what good is a high school degree going to do for me then?

5

Okay. Fine.

6

We were heading into the grocery store when I thought I saw Bob's car drive past. I did a double take but the car was gone. I didn't mention it.

Tommy pushed the cart while I rode gripping to the front, my feet on the frame above the wheels. Mom led us around finding items from her grocery list and placing them in the cart.

After paying, we were carrying the grocery bags out to the car when Tommy said, "There's Bob." Both Mom and I looked across the parking lot and there on the street sat Bob's car. The setting sun cast a glare across the windshield so I couldn't tell if Bob was sitting behind the wheel. Mom started to unlock the trunk and thought better of it. She told us to put the groceries on the floor behind the front seat. We did as told then Tommy said I should take the front seat. That was the first time he ever let me have it without calling it. Mom was already seated when I closed the car door. She had the key in the ignition and had turned it to "on" but she just sat there. I looked over the back of the seat and saw Tommy kneeling on the big bench seat staring out the back window. Finally Mom pushed the clutch in and stepped on the starter. She jiggled the shift lever into reverse and slowly backed out.

"His car is running," Tommy said. Mom shifted to first and aimed for the exit. Once she hit the street, Mom floored it. The sudden acceleration forced me back into my seat, and when she lifted off the gas to speed shift into second I nearly slid to the floor. She took several hard turns that tumbled Tommy and the groceries about the back. Tommy yelled out alerts like "he's still back there" and "you're losing him" and finally "I don't see him anywhere."

It wasn't like we'd lose him for long; even with Mom's roundabout turns, she still drove home. She screeched to a stop and we were out of the car gathering up groceries and hustling them into the house. Mom locked the door while Tommy and I took the bags into the kitchen.

Mom peered through the living room curtains and after several minutes, Bob's green Chrysler crept past. "Shouldn't we call the cops?" Tommy asked. "And tell them what?" Mom retorted. Tommy said to tell them Bob's tailing us but Mom pointed out that there was no law against it. It was just something we were going to have to deal with until he gets bored with us, she said. I didn't like that idea; it made me feel helpless. Playing dead may work for possums, but I thought when most animals tried it, they just got eaten.

Tommy had re-masked the Black Phantom in preparation for the red touch ups. I started to carry some pieces to the back yard when Tommy said "no" he didn't want to take it outside, so without telling Mom, we covered the room with old newspaper, opened the windows and Tommy quietly applied the red paint. "It'll take longer to dry, but we should have it together by the end of the week." I remember it word for word.

Bob was waiting down the street the next morning when Tommy and I headed out for school. Tommy took us the long way around the block so we wouldn't have to pass Bob's car. By the time we returned home that afternoon from school the car was gone. I bounded upstairs and stripped of my school clothes and changed into a pullover and some cutoffs. I was bee lining to the carport when Tommy stopped me. He said we had to do our homework. I protested pointing out that I didn't have any homework; I wanted to take the Western

Flyer out for a ride. Tommy said no and tossed me his Dick and Jane book, *Times and Places*, and said to read it. I'd been getting through *Fun with Dick and Jane* with no problem but *Times and Places*? I flipped through several pages and could barely read half the words. I told him I couldn't read "practically all the words" (I exaggerated) but Tommy just repeated, "read it."

I didn't read *Times and Places*; I put it off for several years. Instead I put Tommy's book in the bed of my Tonka dump truck and wheeled it around the house. But somehow motoring around the house with the book just wasn't the same. Maybe my little dump truck needed Lucky Strike cigarette smoke to make it run right, or Harry James playing "I've Heard That Song Before" on the radio, or my father's chair blocking the way. Something. Maybe it was just the wrong times and the wrong places. I left Tommy's book in the bed of the dump truck and went upstairs.

The disassembled Phantom waited, silent, yet it seemed to me that it was eager to once again be whole, for Tommy to mount up and for the two of them to run fast, to run free. I noticed that Tommy had gone through most of the nuts and bolts and had cleaned and sorted them in preparation for reassembly. I picked up the handlebars and held them out to arms length just to see what they felt like. I imagined that I was almost flying the magnificent Phantom out on Highway 1, hearing the tires whine on the twisting and turning asphalt, feeling the wind through my hair, smelling the salty sea air. "What are you doing?" Tommy asked from behind me. I told him "Nothing," then asked when we'd begin putting the bike together. "Don't know," he said, "soon." He took the handlebars from me. He went to the window and looked out at the spot where we first spied Bob's car sitting on the street, waiting. "What is it?" I asked. Without turning from his post he simply said, "Nothing."

We didn't see Bob that night or the next morning. But even then, Tommy still wouldn't let me play outside. "Why not?" I pestered. "Because." "What does because mean?" I asked. "A reason thereof," Tommy replied. "What does that mean?" "It means," he said, "I'm bigger than you and Mom left me in charge so what I say goes." I thought of several retorts, "you're not the boss of me," "you can't tell me what to do," "you're not my dad," but I swallowed each one like Caster Oil. So I spent the afternoon rolling Tommy's baseball down the stairs into the dark basement. The ball would hit the first few steps then it would skip one, then two and more the further down it bounced. As hard as I tried I couldn't roll it slowly enough to hit every stair on its way down. Tommy had carried his homework upstairs but I knew he was just sitting, the watcher at the window.

No Bob again the next morning. Mom had said she'd be working late that night, "quarter close" or something like that. I had resolved I wasn't going another day without riding my Western Flyer. So once Tommy took position at the window I slipped down to the basement. I pushed my father's trunk from its spot next to his chair to under one of the windows on the side of the house. I unlatched the window and shinnied out.

Staying close to the house to keep out of Tommy's view I took the Flyer from the carport and walked it around the corner before slinging my leg over and riding off.

Having my own bike and no one to watch over me was remarkably freeing. I felt like I could do anything, go anywhere. But I stayed in the neighborhood. Building up speed, I practiced controlled skids. I rode with one hand off the handlebars. I rode on sidewalks and through the vacant lot where the Mann's house stood before it burned to the ground.

When dusk set in I decided to head back. That's when I spotted Bob driving past. I rode around the block and dropped the bike behind the Goodman's hedge. Bob was parked in the same spot that we'd seen him before. Through the yellowing leaves of the hedge I could see Bob's face in the side mirror as he watched our house. From time to time he'd put

a small curved bottle to his lips and take a swig. I
didn't want him to see me ride up to the house but
I was worried if I didn't get home soon Tommy
would find I'd snuck out. I watched and waited for
as long as I could, and formulated a plan. Then
I righted the Flyer and headed back around the
block.

I stopped at the cross street and waited. Finally a
yellow Buick station wagon idled up our street. As
it passed I pulled in behind it. I followed, keeping
the Buick between Bob's line of sight and me. Then
at the precise moment I swung hard right in to our
driveway and continued to the side of the house. I
slipped through the basement window and latched
it closed.

After replacing my father's trunk I bounded
upstairs. I continued up to our bedroom. Tommy
was at the window. "Bob's back," he said. I said
nothing. Bob stayed out there until Mom's regular
time home had come and gone. Then he revved
his engine and squealed the Chrysler's tires as he
peeled away.

We didn't see Bob Friday morning because
Tommy had us leave through the back door.
We scaled the fence behind the house, skipped
through the neighbor's yard and out to the street
beyond. But that afternoon when we got home
Tommy found a letter stuck in the door jamb. It
was addressed to Mom. I could smell the sweet

oily scent of Vitalis on it. Tommy took the letter upstairs to our room. That was the night of the first phone call.

Friday night when we were growing up was mopping the floors night. Actually it was mopping the linoleum night because we only mopped the kitchen, dining room and bathroom. We each had a job, Mom's little division of labor. Tommy's job was to sweep. Mine was holding the dustpan and emptying it into the trash. Mom's job was the actual mopping. She used a yarn mop and a metal bucket filled with hot water and a capful of Pine-sol. Even now, when I ride in a car with one of those little green tree air fresheners hanging from the rear-view mirror I think of Fridays several years ago and mopping linoleum. Mom would dunk the mop three times in the bucket and wring it out by hand. She would do a small section then repeat the process, always dunking the mop three times before wringing it out.

Tommy and I had carried the dining room chairs into the living room so while I stood sentry with the dustpan Tommy swept under the dining table. Mom was well into mopping the dining room when the phone rang. She put the mop in the bucket and dried her hands on her apron. She lifted the handset. "Hello," she said.

It seemed as though several minutes clicked away before Tommy realized Mom wasn't talking, it probably was no more than twenty seconds, but sometimes even just twenty seconds brushes up against forever. He stopped sweeping. That was when I grew aware something was wrong. "You shouldn't call here," Mom said. Tommy's faced hardened, he looked at me and mouthed "Bob."

"No, I don't think that would be a good idea," Mom said, then she was quiet for a long time. I softly padded to the kitchen door and looked inside. Mom was carved from marble, solid and still, her right hand pressing the phone against her ear and her left arm sculpted across her ribs. The fingers on her left hand clutched the phone cord so tightly her knuckles had gone stone white.

"Hang up," Tommy broke the moment with two words. Mom said, "Please don't call here again." She moved the phone from her ear. I could hear Bob but couldn't make out what he said. Mom closed her eyes for a long moment then Tommy took the phone from her hand and placed the phone's handset in its cradle. Tommy asked what Bob wanted, but Mom didn't answer, she just stood there for a moment, her hand cupped around what had been a telephone. Suddenly she went to the window and closed the blinds. Then she did the same for the living room. When she returned she took the mop from the bucket and splattered it on the floor. She didn't dunk it three times. She didn't wring it out.

I'd just gotten into the tub when the phone rang again. Mom answered it after the second ring. I was towel-drying when the phone rang again for the third time. It rang over twenty times before finally going silent.

I was awake and munching Cheerios the first time the phone rang that Saturday morning. As I lifted the handset following the sixth ring, Mom took the phone from my hand. After saying hello she went rigid. It was Bob again, I could tell. Mom told him to stop calling, then she said, "I'm sorry, but I'm hanging up now." She gently replaced the handset, then went back to her room. She didn't say "good morning" and neither did I.

Bob didn't stop calling. The phone rang every twenty minutes for the next three hours. No one answered the phone. Then when noon came and the phone didn't ring it was like we had just gotten a reprieve from Governor Warren. But we weren't granted a full pardon. The phone began ringing again precisely at three PM. I counted six more times that the phone's ringer angrily cried out when by five o'clock, Mom packed us into the car and we headed out to the theater to see Bob Hope in Son of Paleface.

We'd traveled down Hacienda Avenue a few blocks when through the back window I saw Bob's car turn in to our neighborhood. I told Mom I'd just seen him. She sped up. She pushed the speed limit until she made the turn on Campbell Avenue, the home of the Campbell Theater. Mom found a place to park on South Central, then she whisked us into the theater.

The theater itself had originally been built as a bank but had been converted into a movie house in the late 1930's. I guess during the depression theaters were more profitable than banks. Mom bought a carton of Milk Duds for Tommy and me to share, then found us three seats in the back row near the exit. I preferred to sit right up front and could see plenty of seats available but despite my protests Mom refused to move.

Both Mom and Tommy scanned the faces of the patrons as they entered the theater. I knew they were looking for Bob, so I joined in. From what I could see, Bob was a no show, at least until the lights went down and the Looney Tunes cartoon began.

Bob Hope did seem a bit old to have just graduated from Harvard. I guess he was about fifty at the time. I enjoyed the movie, especially Roy Rogers and Trigger, but Mom didn't laugh once. The film was about half over when Mom hustled us out.

The drive home seemed quick and quiet. I expected to see Bob's car parked down the street and was relieved that it wasn't. Inside the house, the phone, which had taken on the role of enemy, remained silent – waiting. Tommy and I went upstairs to bed. In the deadly quiet of night I either awoke or dreamt I did and saw Tommy sitting by the window, staring into the darkness.

Tommy was still asleep when I descended from the top bunk early Sunday morning. Downstairs was quiet; I was the first one up. In the kitchen I started to get out the milk and cereal but decided I'd rather have pancakes instead. So I took the box of Bisquick (A World of Baking in a Box) from the cabinet and set it on the counter as a not-so-subtle hint to Mom.

I took a peek out the window, no Bob thank goodness. I could feel hope rising like the warm morning sun that I would be able to take the Western Flyer out and soar like a red arrow over quiet neighborhood streets.

I tiptoed back into my room to keep from waking Tommy. I gathered up the clothes I wore the day before and went into the bathroom to get dressed. Afterward I went downstairs and sat on the front steps waiting for the rest of the house to awaken.

I watched the garage door rise on the Nelson's house across the street. Mr. Nelson had on a suit and tie. He backed their 1950 Chevy Deluxe, the Styleline model, out of the garage, then he got out and closed the garage door. He got back behind the wheel and waited. The Nelson's had a son, but he'd gone off to college. When he did, Mr. Nelson traded their old four-door 1946 Chevy Stylemaster Town

Sedan for the upgraded two-door Deluxe now idling in the driveway. I guess they were a Chevy Family. Mrs. Nelson emerged from the front door in a flower print dress with matching hat. They were heading off to church. I think they were Catholics.

I watched the Nelson's drive away when I noticed a glint of light coming from the street. I couldn't tell what it was so I left the porch and strolled out to the road.

It was broken glass. I knelt and investigated. At one point the glass had been two bottles of Seagram's 7. The shape and color looked to be the same brand I'd seen Bob drinking from as I hid behind the Goodman's hedge. I was sure the broken glass hadn't been there the day before. Sometime during the night Bob had come back.

When I stood and turned back to the house, Tommy was standing on the porch, hands on his hips. As I approached I debated on telling him about the broken bottles. I didn't tell him and he didn't ask; he already knew. I passed through the door and could smell coffee percolating. Mom was up.

She let me stir the pancake batter while she heated up the griddle. Mom slapped a dollop of Crisco on the griddle using her spatula — I called it a pancake turner-over — to spread the shortening around. Mom always made perfect four-inch cakes, four at a time. Tommy got the first four and I got the next four. We ate them with margarine and real maple syrup, which was expensive so we couldn't use too much.

Once Mom sat down with her pancakes, just two of them, I asked if I could take the Flyer out after breakfast. I think she started to say yes, but before the words escaped she gave a quick glance to Tommy. I missed what he did, but Mom swallowed her words and exchanged them for, "We'll see."

I hated "we'll see." "We'll see," dangled a yes in front of you that was always just out of reach. It was like looking at yes through a window while being stuck in a room of no. "We'll see," teased of possibility but in the end, it had always meant "no."

The phone started ringing at quarter past eleven; Bob had a late night. We all looked at each other. We knew it was Bob calling but Mom went to the phone all the same, decorum and the possibility of "what if?" too strong to ignore. She said, "Hello?"

When he called again, we tried our best to disregard the ringing phone. Tommy went to Mom and they had a brief conversation. Then Mom called out to me saying I should "go outside and ride your bike." I obeyed.

I feel strange looking back on that day. I was sure that during their conference they had decided that as long as Bob kept calling he wouldn't be in our neighborhood, so I was fine playing outside. And I remember as I pedaled down the street that I was glad Bob was calling over and over again because it meant I was free to ride the Flyer. But now, well if he hadn't started calling in the first place and all of the rest, I would have been free to ride anytime I wanted. It makes me think of a prisoner being grateful for tiny whiffs of normalcy, of freedom, when, if things had happened differently he could have had all the freedom he wanted. Being denied that freedom made me appreciate it as the sun warmed my back and the wind tossed my hair. But all in all I wish I had never been in a position to know the freedom I was missing. I hope to never be again.

I tried to stay out through lunch, but hunger hammered away at my resolve finally weakening it into submission. I eventually returned home just before two o'clock. When I walked through the door I could tell the day had left Mom frazzled. She got up and took the phone off the hook. Then she covered it with a dishtowel. The rest of Sunday was silent.

Bob had taken over our lives. The next day Mom called in sick. She had just gotten up, made the call and returned the phone to its place under the dishtowel. Then she went back to bed.

Tommy continued having us leave for school out the back door and wending through the neighbor's yard. We didn't see Bob on the way to school, but

at lunch I saw him drive past the school. He had
the convertible top up even though the day had been
mostly sunny and dry. I saw him drive past the
main entrance then turn and cruise slowly by the
play fields. I looked for Tommy but didn't see him.
I held the news until after school when we were
walking home.

"I saw Bob drive by the school at lunch," I said
to Tommy. "Where?" he asked. "At school." He
clarified that he wanted to know if Bob had gone in
to the parking lot. I told him no that Bob just drove
past. Tommy decided to run home so we did.

When we got close to our house Tommy slowed
to a stop. Bob's car was not there. Tommy seemed
relieved and told me not to tell Mom about seeing
Bob. I asked why not. He said he didn't want to
worry her. I didn't tell her and Bob didn't show
any more that day. But the phone started ringing
again, once at 8:00 and again at 8:15. After it
stopped ringing, Tommy took the phone off the
hook.

Bob's car was back out front first thing the
following morning. Tommy was already up
and dressed when I awoke; he was watching out
the window. "When did he get here?" I whispered.
Tommy didn't turn, just said "about an hour
ago." I asked if Mom was up and Tommy said
he thought so but she was being pretty quiet. At
first I wondered if she was trying to keep from

awakening us but then I realized she probably knew Bob was outside and she was dressing in the dark.

I slid off the top bunk landing with a thump. Seconds later Mom was at the bedroom door. "This has got to stop," she said while pointing at the window. Tommy asked what she was going to do. "I don't know," she answered.

We heard a car start up. It wasn't Bob. It was the '39 Ford with the teenager from up the street behind the wheel. He gave Bob a long look as he drove past. Bob fired up the Chrysler and pulled away with a chirp.

I got dressed and bounced downstairs. I poured some Cheerios and milk in a bowl for breakfast. Then Tommy and I actually left for school by the front door. I didn't see Bob at school and he wasn't there when we got home.

I asked Tommy if I could ride, but he didn't answer. He went down to the basement. I followed and watched him from the steps. He grabbed two screwdrivers, one flat and one Phillips and we went back upstairs. He went to the phone and I watched as he took its cover off. Inside there were wires and magnets and things that even today I couldn't identify. But I did recognize the ringer. It was a simple metal dome with an electric operated clapper inside. Tommy took the Phillips screwdriver and removed the metal dome. He then unscrewed the brass clapper from its bakelite arm. Then he replaced the cover. "Won't that keep it from working?" I asked. Tommy picked up the handset and held it to my ear; I heard the dial tone. "We can call out, it just won't ring," Tommy said. He took the parts up to our room; we never did replace them.

When Mom came home that evening she said things should be fine, that she talked to Bob at work and he understands. We didn't tell her about the phone. We didn't know if Bob understood or not, but it was nice to have a quiet night.

The next day, Wednesday, did seem like Bob had finally gotten the message and moved on. He wasn't there in the morning. I didn't see him at school. I could tell Tommy had his doubts so I didn't even try to ask him about taking out the Flyer. I asked if he wanted to reassemble the Black Phantom but Tommy said not right now. When Mom came home she looked like she had a question on her lips (any sign of Bob?) but it went unasked. We tried to have a relaxing evening but were unsuccessful. At 8:00 Mom turned and stared at the phone even though it was silent. At 8:15 she did the same thing. And again fifteen minutes later and fifteen minutes after that. The phone couldn't ring, but it almost didn't matter. We were still on edge.

I was up before Tommy and as had become my

routine, looked out the window for Bob. He wasn't there, but I could see a another broken bottle on the street, right next to where Bob's car door would be. I knew he been outside sometime during the night.

Tommy had overslept and we had to rush out for school. When he steered me to the back door I knew Tommy had already known that Bob had returned. On the way to school Tommy told me Bob had shown up around 4:00 AM and sat there in his car with the engine running for about twenty minutes. Then he tossed a bottle out the window and took off. That was the last time Bob parked outside our house. We didn't see him anymore that day or the next morning. Then came Friday night.

7

It was late when Bob rapped on the door. Tommy was at our bedroom window as soon as the first knuckle hit the wooden door. "It's Bob," he said. I heard Mom go to the door and tell Bob to go away. Bob said he just wanted to talk, to apologize. Tommy and I watched from the top of the stairs as Mom opened the front door. Bob was crying and Mom let him in. She gave us the look and we went back to our room.

We could hear them but not what they were saying. There were times it got so quiet all I could hear was the steady ticking of the alarm clock. I stuck my head over the side of my bed to ask Tommy if he could hear anything but Tommy shushed me with a finger to his lips. Then I could hear them again. The tone of Bob's voice varied from almost whispering to pleading and whining to loud and aggressive. Then we heard what sounded like tussling. Tommy headed for the stairs but I whispered, "Wait, you'll get into trouble." He went anyway. He was back before I could climb down from the top bunk and he grabbed the forks to the Black Phantom.

Tommy was at the bottom of the stairs when I got to the top. I could see that Bob had Mom bent over the arm of the loveseat, a handful of her hair was twisted in his fat hand and he was pushing her face into the cushion. The bottom of Mom's dress was pulled up over her back and Bob was pushing his hips into her. Bob let out a strange yell just as Tommy got there with the forks. Bob raised his head and Tommy hit him in the forehead with the forks. Bob was stunned, but Tommy had pulled his swing at the last second. Bob was up now, pants down around his knees. He tried stepping toward Tommy but he lost his balance. Tommy had the neck of the forks in both hands, the same grip he used in the Junior Hardball League, he stepped into his swing, power coming from his legs and hips and he smashed the forks into Bob's head. Bob was out as he fell into the coffee table. His head cracked against the table and slammed his jaw into his chest. Tommy dropped the bent forks and went to Mom, her face still in the cushion. Bob never moved.

Tommy turned to me and yelled to get back upstairs. At first I couldn't move, but Tommy's fierce narrow gaze got me going. From my bed I could hear Mom and Tommy talking. Then it grew quiet. After some time I heard rustling and grunting and the front door open. I looked out the bedroom window and saw Mom and Tommy drag Bob out to his car. They strained to get him in the passenger seat. Tommy went 'round the back of the house while Mom went through Bob's pockets. Mom found Bob's car keys and started the car. Tommy came back wheeling my bright red Western Flyer. Together they loaded the bicycle into the back seat. Mom started the big convertible while Tommy wedged himself in the back beside the Flyer. They drove with the headlights off into the night.

I went downstairs and straightened up as best I could. I picked up the bent forks and carried them upstairs. I placed the one undamaged fork on the floor and holding it in place with my feet, I pulled on the bent fork in an effort to true it up. After several attempts I got it pretty straight. I put the front wheel in the forks and gave it spin to see of it would work. It looked like it had never been damaged.

I set out to reassemble the beautiful Black Phantom. I carefully pulled the wrench and turned the screwdriver. I greased the ball bearings and adjusted the front hand brake. I polished the chrome and buffed off any fingerprints. I checked for any leftover pieces, but every nut, bolt and screw were accounted for. The fire red and gloss black Phantom looked like it had just arrived from the factory. And I felt...relief. I didn't know what it was then, but that's what it was, relief.

It was after three o'clock in the morning when I stood there staring at the mighty Phantom. Still, Mom and Tommy had not come home. I went downstairs and for some reason I covered the loveseat with a spare white sheet. Then I sat down to wait.

Up in her room Mom's alarm clock went off at six, but she wasn't there to shut it off and the spring wound down to silence. I'd fallen asleep. I went to the window. The milkman had made his rounds so I went out to the porch and gathered up the two glass bottles he'd left. That's when I saw Tommy pedaling slowly up the street. Mom sat on the bike's seat, her head resting on Tommy's back. Tommy coasted and then braked to a stop on the grass. Neither was strong enough to steady the bicycle and lower it's kickstand so they just let it drop to the ground. I stood aside as they entered the house. Tommy went straight upstairs but Mom stopped and took in the house; last night's mess gone, the loveseat covered by a slept on sheet. She cupped my face with her left hand then she softly walked away and drew a bath.

I put the milk in the fridge. I ascended the stairs and could hear Mom quietly washing. Tommy was on his bed. He looking like he'd been used up and wrung out. "Where'd you go?" I asked him. "Highway 9." "Where's Bob?" I asked. Tommy just turned and faced the wall.

It was three days later when I'd heard on the radio that there had been a single car accident on Highway 9 in the hills outside of Saratoga, one fatality. A county sheriff had noticed the damage to the cliff edge where the car had gone over. The driver had been thrown from the green Chrysler convertible and had sustained severe head injuries. Next of kin were being notified.

Tommy never said anything about the reassembled Black Phantom, and he never rode her. When he did ride (which wasn't often) he returned to riding the red Western Flyer, as if he'd never given it to me and it had always been his. I had a hard time at first riding the Phantom because I was too short to reach the pedals while seated. I had to ride standing up, swaying from side to side each time the pedal reached it's lowest point.

Tommy was never the same. It was like he'd crossed into an alternate universe in a Ray Bradbury story. He would do as he was told, but nothing more. It was like his entire will, every motivation, every desire was wound up in that powerful swing of the Black Phantom's forks and he had nothing left. He didn't even come downstairs that following summer when Mom brought Frank home from the hospital. Tommy didn't hate Frank; he just didn't have anything to do with him.

Tommy didn't go with me that summer or any of the following ones when Mom put me on the Greyhound to my grandparents' house. Tommy didn't play baseball during the summers, he didn't hang out with friends or ask about diving for abalone. He didn't do much at all. He'd read and when we finally got a television he'd sit and stare at it.

I think that's why Mom moved us here to Cloverdale, thinking maybe it would help Tommy. I brought the Phantom, but Mom left the loveseat behind. Funny but she still brought my father's chair. It's in the storage shed out behind our house with the Black Phantom along with my father's footlocker and amber ashtray, as if one day he'll return.

She told some people he had returned for a few weeks in the fall of 1952 and that was how she explained Frank. None of us ever spoke of that night and her fabrication about my father's return were the last rites over the burial of an awful night.

I stopped going down to see Grandma and Grandpa after I found a letter they'd written to

Mom after Frank was born. The letter said they thought she should send Tommy and me to live with them. They accused Mom of losing her way and blamed her for what Bob had done to her. They thought Tommy and me should be spared exposure to her evil ways. They'd wanted nothing to do with her, yet she still sent me down to visit. That was confusing, but not as confusing as the way her own parents had treated Mom. It surprised me after my grandfather died in '63 when the box of wetsuits came in the mail. But by then they were just shadows of a better time.

Moving here didn't change a thing for Tommy. We lost him in 1952 and physically moving wasn't going to alter that. We'd have to go back in time to make things right, but since Einstein died ten years ago, there's no hope of time travel.

"Let's go play catch," I'd offer, but Tommy was never in the mood. "I got a couple of quarters, we can ride into town and get some fries," I'd say but he wasn't hungry. We grew more apart once Tommy hit junior high and we went to different schools. By high school it seemed like Tommy and me were more like roommates than brothers. I stopped trying and I feel shame for it.

Tommy took a job working graveyard at the grocery store after graduating high school. He did that for a little over two years when last Christmas he bought himself a present, a 32-caliber revolver.

For his twenty-first birthday he gave himself a bullet. I wish I had known how to help him.

Frank found the body. Tommy had taken the blood red and gloss black Phantom out of the shed and set it resting on its kickstand. Then he sat down with his back against the shed and put the muzzle to his temple. He'd been dead for several hours when Frank noticed the Phantom in the yard. He said he'd been quiet when he went looking for me, thinking Tommy was still asleep in his room. He said the gun had fallen from Tommy's grasp. Christ he's only eleven, but Frank said he didn't touch a thing before he ran to the house to phone the police. I don't know what happened to the gun.

9

Just so you know, I plan on destroying this after you've read it. Maybe I'll burn it or tear it to little scraps. I've done as you asked and I don't feel the slightest difference. The sun still rises on a world where someone can follow and terrorize you at will, where parents still blamed their daughters for being raped, where children are conceived in violence and where Tommy is still dead.

I don't know how Tommy felt. I've never killed a man, even for the best of reasons. But had it been me, I'd have done exactly what Tommy had. Would I have been better able to live with it? Maybe. I would have had a big brother to help me through it. In the end, all Tommy had was me. I think I'll stop here.

DEPARTMENT MEMORANDUM

FROM: Analyst Danielle Peterson
TO: Det. Ron Steele
SUBJECT: Results of Manuscript Analysis

This analyst conducted a review of details found within the body of the aforementioned manuscript. Two Henry J's were found as part of the 1965 graduating class at Cloverdale High School. One whose last name began with the letter 'J' and one whose middle initial was 'J.'

The latter did have an older brother name of Thomas who also attended Cloverdale High School. There were no records of a Frank also attending the same high school for any of the subsequent six years. There was a Frank with the same last name enrolled in the elementary school at the time in question.

Assuming this is the correct Henry J, a thorough records search was conducted regarding the individuals in question.

1. Police records show that Thomas died of a self-inflicted gunshot wound in January 1965.

2. County records indicate that Henry J's mother died of pancreatic cancer June 1969.

3. Draft records show Henry J registered for the draft in 1965, but was not called into service. Further, draft records show Frank was drafted in 1972 and received wounds in Viet Nam. Frank was awarded a purple heart. Military records also show that Frank died of ethanol poisoning March 1984.

4. Sheriff records for Santa Clara County (location of Saratoga, CA) were negative for any single car accidents in the September/October 1952 time frame that occurred on Highway 9.

5. Sheriff records for Santa Cruz County (adjacent to Santa Clara County) reveal a single car accident that was reported Monday 29 September 1952. A Robert Heller was deceased on the scene. Vehicle involved was a green 1948 Chrysler Convertible.

6. Town of Duncan's Landing Police records indicate Henry J was briefly held and released in 1981.

7. Following the police records, there are no further public records for Henry J. Social Security, all three credit agencies, voter registration, and DMV are all negative for the individual in question.

Please contact me if you have further needs.

Cloverdale Police Dept.

112 Broad St.

Cloverdale, CA 94525

Ms. Jennifer Haley

413 N Jefferson St.

Cloverdale, CA 94525

Re: Manuscript.

Dear Ms. Haley:

Enclosed is the manuscript you provided. After thorough analysis of the events and descriptions outlined in the manuscript, the department has determined that the manuscript, although very detailed, is a work of fiction. The department would like to thank you for your concern and for your sense of civic responsibility.

Sincerely

Ron Steele

Detective Ronald Steele

78

PART TWO: BROKEN RECORD

I read the news today...

For years it seemed like it never really changed, just the same news with different names and different places, like the photos in the picture frame section of Wal-Mart--black four-by-sixes, gold eight-by-tens, silver two-by-threes of the same black and white blonde Vaseline smile. It didn't matter what day it was, it didn't matter where I was living, it didn't matter the season or the year, the news was always the same--national news, local news, editorials, features, sports, comics. Who tried, who lied, who cried, who died; just the same and the same.

But today was different. The change wasn't the apartment, which was just the last in a string of apartments all clones of each other like fruit flies, differentiated only by the number on the door. It wasn't the aging table and chair, bare wood graying like an old dog, faithfully following me from town to town and place to place. It wasn't the coffee, black and acrid regardless of the color of the can it came in. It was the news...and me.

Today I sat down with a cup of black coffee at the small drop-leaf table in the small kitchen of my equally small apartment to read the newspaper and when I looked up I found myself staring at rusty wrought iron embracing the Gates of Heaven Cemetery. Driving the hundred miles from my apartment to the Gates of Heaven had been a sip of bitter coffee. I set the parking brake of my pick-up and cut off the engine. I put the newspaper on the seat and rolled down the window. Tender morning air leaked in, towing the faint smell of grass and dust and exhaust. All was still and silent with no breeze or bird to plague the eternal rest of the dead. Time itself walked on tip toes quietly skirting around the rows of headstones and markers. Could it be right that the Gate to Heaven was a small unkempt cemetery?

The Gates of Heaven sat on the side of a hill and looked down a gentle slope watching over a copse of trees. The trees graced a small cliff and fed off a clear running stream. The stream was a Wyeth painting of trees and bushes, sprinkled with debris and broken pieces of concrete. The water cut into the land wielding time and erosion to create the earthen walls of a creek. The umber walls rose in height to about ten feet. The dirt cliff, fathered by ages of flowing water, was dark and straight.

I opened the door and slid out of the truck. I gently closed the door and heard it latch. The morning sun was warm, warmer that I expected, and it promised comfort. False promises. The dry air smelled exactly as it had so many years earlier, of dying grasses watered unwontedly by saline tears. The only sound was the gravel crunching under my boots; even the ghosts stopped their amaranthine whispering when I passed through the gates.

I read the news today...for years it seemed like it never really changed; or was it just me? The grave was smaller than I remembered. I should have expected that. Memories don't seem to adjust proportionately with age. While remembering, I'm always seven going on eight. I'm always seven going on eight and I'm in the woods looking for the perfect tree to climb.

President Reagan was shot that year. But for all I knew it was a ray gun that was shot that year. Some guy named Hinckley shot a ray gun in 1981.

I think that guy Hinckley was destined to shoot a ray gun because he was born with a name that sounded like what was wrong with

him. His thoughts were all hiked up and wrinkled and twisty...
they were Hinckleyed.

When I was seven going on eight I loved climbing trees. They
called to me like sirens huddled together on windswept Homeric
rocks. But, to climb, you had to find the right ones. Young trees
and dead trees were eliminated outright. The lowest branch had
to evoke Robert Browning, high enough that if you jumped with
all your might you could just grab it. Then you would hook your
ankle over the limb and pull yourself up. The tree couldn't have
vast sections without branches because that would defeat the goal:
to get up as high as possible and still be able to get down without
the help of the fire department. There were a wide variety of trees
to choose from: fir, hemlock, spruce, cedar, oak, and maple. And
deodar cedar trees with sap nodules on the branches just under
a thin layer of bark that popped like pimples when you grabbed
them. The sap wouldn't wash off and it took about a week for it
to wear away. I climbed them twice, their lure stronger than my
memory.

There were even a few old redwoods that somehow had survived
the loggers' saw. The redwoods towered over the other trees and
I knew if I could climb one to the very top I could touch Skylab.
But the lowest branches were at least thirty feet up; they may have
well been a mile. Skylab was safe from my fingerprints.

When I finally reached the top of the tree I would take a long
look to survey the territory. Man, I loved climbing trees. It was
my world. I loved the expansive view, and hiding in the leaves,
and just being above everything alone with my thoughts. It was
devolutionary.

I have not climbed trees since that summer of 1981. I guess I did not want to be alone with my thoughts.

But today I stand alone with my thoughts in a mostly forgotten cemetery that had once been watered by mostly forgotten tears.

Once you truly know something you can never un-know it, and it seems as though you've always known it. You have always known, always will know and can't really remember not knowing. It's the weight of true knowledge.

I'm not talking learning, like how to figure sines, cosines and tangents. That's not knowledge because no one ever knows how to figure those. It's just words in a borrowed page of a loaned textbook that you return at the end of the semester. It's not yours, never was, never will be. It's just your name at the bottom of a long list of other names in a book that belongs to nobody.

In everyone's life there is a moment...a time...a decision you make or fail to make that changes the entire direction of your life. My moment was not here in this cemetery in front of this grave. For me it happened about thirty years ago when I was seven going on eight. I was on my knees up in the attic.

But that's not where the story starts. As I remember, it starts...

Saturday, August 29

..here: Portola Avenue, a tree-lined street in Duncan's Landing, a blink of a town in northern California; not a sidewalk in sight.

When I was seven going on eight I owned a mutt of a bicycle. It was pathetic. Wheels didn't match, forks, seat, handlebars all unwanted leftovers from other bikes. And it was all my own doing. It was my creation and I its Doctor Frankenstein. But it worked and it was mine. And wouldn't you know someone would steal my bike after just a few months. Hell if I knew someone was desperate enough to steal that dog turd, I would have given it to 'em.

Summer vacation was winding down but not so fast that the pending weight of school squashed all hopes for unplanned days. Loose threads from my cutoffs tickled my thighs while I pedaled my bike down Portola Avenue. My shirt was coming apart at the seams underneath the arms, but I appreciated the venting during the hot summer days. My tennis shoes were tattered and decomposing in a slow Keds death. I had to wrap silver duct tape around one to keep the rubber sole and the canvas upper from divorcing.

When I was seven going on eight Portola Avenue was really nothing more than middle class, a middle class that even then was fading away like an old photograph of those who had dreamt it, but to me it was Oz. Big gabled jewel houses with detached garages--some big enough for two cars--and manicured yards with golden oaks and emerald pines standing guard. I could smell the pine flavored with a hint of freshly cut grass. Up the street a brown metallic 1972 Chevy Caprice Classic station wagon pulled in to the driveway of perfection. I heard the engine fall silent and the ratcheting click, click, click of the parking brake as Mrs. Brownsberger pressed it to the floor. She and her daughter got out. Mrs. Brownsberger was named Jean or Jane; I can't remember which. I should remember. Her name should stick with me like a popcorn husk between my molars. How can I not remember?

"Hey Jimmy."

I looked down at my ratty shoes. I stopped pedaling and coasted, strategically using the sprocket to hide the duct tape.

"Hey," I said.

That was Karen. She and I went to school together. Karen Brownsberger was an eight-year-old porcelain doll. Her face came to a point at her chin and it made me think of a teardrop on its way up to heaven. She wore her brown wavy hair short. Her mouth was small and when she was happy, her pale cerulean eyes smiled.

Karen and her mother had been to the Lucky grocery store on the other side of town--'Everyday Low Prices'. Lucky's low prices made them popular but they disappeared altogether a number of years ago in a chess game of corporate takeovers. Checkmate. I slowly rolled by and watched Karen and her mother lift the paper bags of Lucky groceries from the back of the station wagon. I put pressure to the pedals and picked up speed. I was heading for home. My neighborhood was but a half a mile from Portola Avenue but it was a whole world away from Karen.

Karen and I had been best friends during kindergarten and first grade and part way through second grade...until I got my first lesson in peer pressure. Apparently in second grade boys aren't supposed to like girls. The boys were convinced, despite all medical data to the contrary, that cooties were contagious. And those with cooties were banned like biblical lepers. So although I liked Karen and she was fun to play with, I caved to the pressure like I was made of wet papier mâché. I stopped playing with her and we rarely even spoke. I miss her.

Compared to Portola Avenue my street may as well have been in Bangladesh. The block of houses was a worn out, used up, tossed aside gaggle of 1930's matchstick military houses, too old and neglected to stand at attention. They sagged at ease. Even the lawns had given up and packed it in. Smart Gables? Nope. Tall stately trees? Nuh unh. Garages? Please. People parked on the street or on the dirt where lawns were rumored to have once been.

At the end of the block was a stand of rusting mailboxes. "Stand" may be too generous a word. It was a four by four post planted in the dirt with a six-foot long two-by-four tacked on top, probably nailed there by the Army Corps of Engineers when the world was in black and white. The mailboxes themselves may have been all uniform during previous lifetimes, but in their current incarnation they were a mishmash of sizes and shapes. The only thing uniform was the rust.

As I road my bike past the mailboxes, the Crazy Lady was busy rifling through them, wearing her standard ensemble of faded house dress and worn slippers under a tussle of wild, ratted hair. She had to have been well into in her seventies and twice a year she ran an orange rinse through her hair so it seemed to be in a constant state of long gray roots and scorched orange ends. The Crazy Lady came out and checked her mailbox about ten times a day; including a few times even after the mail had come and she had collected it up and carried it into her house. That by itself should have been enough to earn her nickname. But she also checked everybody else's mailbox, often mixing up everyone's cards and letters and bills. I don't know who first dubbed her the Crazy Lady but everyone I knew referred to her by that title, right down to the capital letters. I didn't call her the Crazy Lady, at least not out loud. I didn't call her anything.

I stopped my bike in front of the oldest house on the block, Henry's house. Henry's house was built in the teens, before the rest of the neighborhood came to fight the depression. Henry's house never knew the word renovation. The house still had real fuses, blowing with regularity in a soot-stained fuse-box in the one car garage. My mom and I were living with my Uncle Henry, my father's brother, at the time and had been for a while. I dropped the bike there in the soft dry dirt of the yard and scampered up a few wooden stairs and was engulfed by the house.

Here was the real estate brochure for Uncle Henry's house: This enchanting (tiny) two bedroom/one bath home with original charm (nothing had been done to it including paint since before

Franklin Roosevelt and steel pennies, there was even a chicken coop out back from God-knows-when) offers a living room with fireplace and warm (warm in the summer maybe) hardwood floors throughout. It also boasts a cozy (tiny) kitchen and bonus room (my room, it was maybe a closet or pantry or sewing room at one time; 'tiny' was actually too big a word to describe it, I could barely fit a mattress in there). Enjoy the charming front porch (there was a cover over the steps) and mountain views (if you stand on the roof). Close to shops (then the Sunshine Supermarket – now a Circle K) & restaurants (then – the Truck Stop, now – the Truck Stop) in a quiet & natural (weeds) setting.

I wandered into the empty house. Just inside the front door was a small landing with a coat closet. Beyond was the living room. The room was furnished with an old hide-a-bed that must have weighed two thousand pounds. It sagged in the middle like a swayback mule. The hide-a-bed had been bright green at one point. Well, it was still green; a worn out faded green, but you had to look under an off-white slipcover to know that. The room also had two mismatched easy chairs, a beanbag chair, a pile of throw pillows in the far corner and a big wooden spool that we called a coffee table, which had most likely been stolen from the phone company. The coffee table had once occupied a spot in the middle of the room, but had been shoved aside to accommodate the hide-a-bed when my mother and I moved in.

The hide-a-bed stood open and unmade. That was where my mother slept. Sometimes she was "Mom," and other times "Mary." She answered to both and I used them interchangeably. I straightened the sheets and blankets, then folded, levered and put the bed away. A tail of sheet peeked out from the transformed bed but it was good enough. I replaced the cushions.

Beyond the living room were stairs leading to the bathroom and two bedrooms that were built over the garage, and a small hallway. My room was off the hallway and the kitchen stood at the end of the hall. Past the kitchen were the laundry room and the back door. I went upstairs to take a leak.

The bathroom was a guy's bathroom. It was painted dark blue and had not a single piece of pastel themed artwork on the walls. The shower curtain was industrial rubber just like those used in cheap roadside motels. There was no crystal container of multi-colored heart-shaped soaps. No fuzzy carpet on the toilet; heck, no fuzzy carpet on the floor. No Glade Air Freshener on the sink, just a bar of Lava hand soap. No holder for the roll of toilet paper, it sat on the windowsill. And the toilet didn't even have a cover for the tank. Well, it had a cover, but we had to take it off so often to get the flapper to seal or to free the chain on the lever or to bend the float to keep the toilet from running, that eventually the cover found a nice retirement spot behind the sink.

I zipped up after my whiz and didn't wash my hands because; one, I didn't pee on myself and; two, no one else was home.

I went downstairs to make some lunch. The kitchen had white tile counter tops with mold colored grout. The upper cabinets had windowed doors so that even God could see that none of the dinnerware matched. The lower cabinets and the pantry had regular doors. The prehistoric refrigerator had an upper freezer that needed to be defrosted every so often. I liked defrosting the freezer because the built up ice scrapped off in a fine powder like snow. It was about the only time we ever saw snow in that part of

California. There was a turquoise blue gas stove with pilot lights that never worked. You used a match to light the burners on the stove, and had to get on your knees and use a flaming rolled up newspaper to light the oven.

I got out the Lady Lee saltines and Lady Lee peanut butter from the pantry. Lady Lee was the Lucky store brand, the cheap stuff. The peanut butter didn't contain hydrogenated vegetable oil, which the expensive brands like Jiff and Skippy had, so the peanut oil would rise to the top and I was forced to mix it in with a butter knife. Nowadays they call that "All Natural" and you pay extra for it. I spread some peanut butter over a few saltine crackers. I capped them with another saltine and bit into my peanut butter and cracker sandwich.

"Jimmy!"

That was Wayne.

Wayne was outside in the yard by my bike. Even though there was still a third of summer left, he wore a winter coat tied around his waist. He always had that winter coat with him, either on or tied around his waist. Wayne was a year or so older than I was, but in street-years he would have been in his mid-teens. He was a few inches taller than me. His light brown hair looked like he combed it with his fingers. Wayne had an angel face and warm smile. He was probably a sociopath. I went to the door still munching away and holding a couple of cracker sandwiches.

"'Sup Wayne?" I said blowing cracker dust.

"Give me a ride to the Sunshine Super."

I answered with a shrug, stepped outside and closed the door to the house. I handed a cracker sandwich to Wayne. Wayne put the whole thing in his mouth and crunched down.

"What are you buying?" I asked.

"Nothin'."

Wayne would have a rap sheet as long as the Old Testament... if he ever got caught, which to my knowledge he never had. If there ever was a born thief and vandal it was Wayne. I'll bet there's graffiti in his mother's womb.

I mounted my bike while Wayne climbed onto the handlebars and we set off riding double.

"Don't go through the field," Wayne said.

We usually cut through the field thereby saving about ten minutes. But the bumps and rocks were murder on your ass if you had it wedged on the handlebars of a bicycle. We stuck to the dusty streets of Duncan's Landing.

Even though Wayne was older than I by over a year, we were in the same grade. He got "held back" as we say now, in the second grade. I was no academic wonder, but second grade wasn't what I would have called work. It seemed to me that all it took to pass was to put your time in like a prisoner waiting for parole. Learning about sentences and capitalization was like marking an X on the calendar. Spelling was prison laundry. Geography was eating gruel with the other inmates. Arithmetic was introduction to word problems (if prisoner Jimmy had four apples that he wanted to share with fellow cons Wayne and Karen, how many would each get after Wayne pulled his shiv?). Second grade was the time spent between recesses. I couldn't fathom having to do two stretches in second grade. Second grade--Christ.

"Wayne? How'd you flunk second grade?" I cross-examined.

I turned into the small market and stopped in front of the Sunshine Supermarket.

"I was sick," Wayne said as he hopped off the bike and slipped the winter coat on.

"What of?"

Wayne ran up to the door of the store, opened it and hollered back at me.

"School!"

I followed Wayne into the Sunshine Supermarket. A young female clerk with hawk eyes stood behind the cash register and watched us like we were two plump field mice.

Wayne was browsing the aisles of the store looking at Star Wars action figures and the like. I wandered down the candy aisle. I didn't have any money so I just noted their selection. My favorite was Butterfingers; they were chocolaty, crunchy, peanut buttery goodness. The Nestle Company had just acquired Butterfingers from the Curtiss Candy Company but Curtiss couldn't find the original recipe so Nestle had to make up their own. While I was quite a Butterfingers connoisseur, at the time my expert opinion was that I didn't notice a difference. My mom liked Junior Mints and Mountain Bars.

Wayne made his way over to the cigar section and looked around.

"C'mere," Wayne said.

I left the aisle of chocolate heaven and joined him.

"What?"

"See these?" Wayne said.

I didn't answer; I didn't know the word 'rhetorical' but I knew some questions didn't need to be answered. Wayne was in front of a huge display of cigars. I took in a deep breath, savoring the smell.

"Just look at them awhile," Wayne said. "Take some out and smell them under your nose...like this."

Wayne rolled a cigar under his nose and inhaled deeply.

"Keep doing it until she makes you stop," Wayne nodded toward the clerk.

Wayne zipped up his coat. I knew something was up, but I didn't know what.

"Okay," I said.

I looked at the display of cigars. Rows and rows of small brown torpedoes sardined in boxes with gold lettering that looked like they were meant for kings. I read the labels: Blackstone, Old Virginia, Old Masters. I took out an Old Virginia and smelled it. It smelled like autumn.

Wayne took a position over near the lighters and cigarettes.

I put the Old Virginia back and picked out a Blackstone. I admired the craftsmanship, the blend of flavor, complexity and aroma. For a moment I was wandering the badlands of Oklahoma on a golden palomino heading for Cimarron, New Mexico territory. I squinted.

By then the clerk had spotted me and was making a direct line to me through the toy section as if she had a straightedge. I picked up a few more cigars.

"Little boy," she said as she blew past Luke Skywalker and Princess Leia. They shuddered from her wake. "You can't buy those."

I didn't say anything.

"Little boy," she said taking the cigars from my hands. Behind her, I saw Wayne hoist a carton of Belair cigarettes up under his coat and then wander back to Darth Vader.

"You can't hang out here. Are you going to buy something?" the clerk said.

"I guess not," I accessoried.

Wayne stole to the door and I followed him out.

That wasn't really the first time I had crossed the line of the law, just the first time I was aware of it. About a month before, Wayne and I had seen "Raiders of the Lost Ark" three times one Thursday afternoon at the Coddingtown multiplex in Santa Rosa. We only paid for the first showing. I didn't know that you weren't allowed to stay and watch the movie over and over. So at the end of the first two shows we exited the theater with the non-criminals and milled around the lobby or went to use the rest room while workers finished sweeping up popcorn and black Jujubes and mopping up spilled Coca Cola and Dr. Pepper from the theater floor. Then the workers let the legal patrons, and illegal Wayne and me, in for the next showing. I was in a different town in a darker world when I later learned the rules.

From the Sunshine Supermarket we pedaled along the road until we got to an overpass that spanned a creek. The creek bordered our neighborhood on the south and west sides. Some creeks had names like Jones Creek or Lost Shoe Creek or Drowned Horse Creek, but our creek had no name. It was just the creek. We dismounted and slid down the side of the overpass where a gap in the chain link fence was just wide enough for two delinquents and a piece-of-shit bike to fit through.

The sun was high over head and heat swells rising from the asphalt road twirled a Marsh Hawk round and round on the hot air. Wayne shrugged off his coat and tied it around his waist. He carried the Belair cigarettes like a trophy.

We walked along the edge of the creek heading to our favorite spot - the rope swing. The fat, natural fiber three-strand-laid rope swing dangled from a thick branch that overhung an especially deep spot of the creek. Someone had drilled a hole through an eighteen-inch wooden plank, laced the rope through, and knotted it off underneath. The swing was tied to a tree that grew on the bank of the creek, its roots on the water side stuck out of the creek wall like bony dead fingers and made a convenient staircase down to the creek bed. I rested my bike against the trunk of the tree.

Wayne sat cross-legged on the ground next to the creek. I sat next to him with my legs over the edge of the embankment resting on skeletal roots. He opened the carton of smokes and took out a pack. Like an old pro he slapped the pack against his palm, packing down the tobacco.

Wayne opened the pack and tapped out a cigarette. He placed it between his lips and dug a book of matches from his pocket. That nine-year-old was as experienced as the Marlboro Man. He opened the matchbook, inside there was but one solitary match. This concerned me because I was looking forward to smoking and being 'cool' and to me only one match meant only one smoker.

"Just one match?" I worried.

"Not a problem," Wayne reassured.

Wayne pulled the match from the book, struck it on the strike pad and with his hands cupped around the flame, lit the cigarette. Wayne inhaled deep and I could hear the tobacco crackle. He then slowly blew smoke. He drew on it a couple of times 'til it was burning well.

Wayne flicked the pack so another cigarette rested partway out. He took out the cigarette and handed me the pack. I watched intently as Wayne pulled the lit cigarette from his lips and replaced it with the fresh one. He pressed the lit end against the unlit cigarette in a fiery kiss and drew smoke to light it. Once lit, he handed the cigarette to me.

I puffed like a steam engine. Wayne blew smoke from his nose. I tried to blow smoke from my nose but accidentally inhaled. This sent spasms through my lungs like an electrical current and I had a coughing jag that brought tears to my eyes. I finally recovered.

"This is cool," I hacked, wiping away the tears.

We smoked and smoked and smoked and smoked and smoked... oh and we smoked.

❅ ❅ ❅

I lit a fresh cigarette from my last butt and ground the stub into the dirt next to a dozen others and the nearly empty pack. Wayne had shinnied up the tree and was crawling on his belly out on the branch to the rope swing, cigarette pressed between his lips.

"Ever seen a Playboy?" Wayne asked, his cigarette bobbing up and down with each word.

"Yeah, I've seen 'em in the rack at the store," I said.

Wayne reached around the branch, grabbed the rope and started to swing it back toward the shore, back toward me.

"I mean seen inside one?" Wayne bobbed, smoke rubbing his eyes.

"No."

"It's got pictures of naked ladies."

I reached for the rope but it was short. It swung away.

"Wow," I exclaimed. "And you can buy them?"

Wayne applied more force to the rope. It swung back and I was able to grab it. I jumped off the edge and mounted the swing and sailed out over the water. Wayne headed back down the branch.

"No, you have to be eighteen," Wayne explained.

"Man, naked ladies and cigarettes. I can't wait to grow up," I marveled.

❋ ❋ ❋

I was trapped amid a clump of bushes facing a hundred invisible poison-dipped spears. My breathing was harsh and heavy, my mind sketching out an escape plan.

"Dr. Jones," Wayne said, "again, we see there is nothing you can possess which I cannot take away. You chose the wrong friends. This time it will cost you."

I curled my lip. "Too bad the Hovitos don't know you the way I do, Belloq," I snarled.

I handed over the golden statue (my cigarette) to the evil Belloq (Wayne).

"Yes, too bad," Wayne smirked. "You could warn them...if only you spoke Hovitos."

With that I took out running toward the edge of the creek and the rope swing.

"Jock," I cried out, "start the engines! Start the engines!"

I jumped off the edge of the creek and grabbed the rope swing. I swung out over the flowing water and, spotting the imaginary seaplane, let go of the rope. I splashed down like a space capsule. The water was cool. A moment later Wayne splashed in next to me.

The pile of cigarette butts had grown. We had almost finished a second pack. I flopped to the ground with the cold sweats. My hand, cigarette clamped between my fingers, quivered in nicotine overdose. I could tell Wayne wasn't doing much better, but he was skilled at hiding it.

"Ugh," I moaned. "I don't know how people can smoke these things."

"Try cigars."

"I'm never smoking again as long as I live."

So far so good.

It was nearly dark by the time I dropped Wayne off at his house. I had passed the 'I don't feel right' stage and had progressed to the 'if I could just throw up I'd feel better' stage about the time Wayne stumbled off the handlebars. I made my way back home. Green and queasy, I dropped my bike in the yard. The house was raucous with music and voices. I ascended the steps and opened the door; a cloud of white, sweet smoke escaped.

As I said we were living with my Uncle Henry. Henry was a kind man and gentle soul... what most of society would deem a sucker, to be succinct. He never had much and never would--but what he had he shared. While I walked through the house, a dozen people in various states of sobriety smiled at me as I passed. Some drank, one drew deeply from a bong, others talked and laughed. Henry's house was always a neon light blazing 'OPEN'. Open to the wretched refuse, the homeless, the tempest-tossed. Emma Lazarus should have put a plaque on his door.

Mary sat at the end of the couch nursing some pale wine, probably Boone's Farm Strawberry Hill. Mother Mary was still in her early twenties; she was just fifteen when I was born. She wore a tired smile and cutoff jeans under her black waitress skirt.

"Jimmy," she said, "come here. You don't look so good."

I decided to tell her about stealing the carton of Belair cigarettes and smoking pack after pack like we were either nicotine junkies or French and that I was feeling cold sweat gathering at my brow like a coming rainstorm and I was about to faint. It came out like this:

"I'm just tired."

"Go get the clothes out of the dryer, I'll be there in a minute," Mom said.

My room was furnished with a twin mattress that occupied most of the floor and two cardboard boxes that held all of my worldly possessions. I had a small orange desk lamp, which I kept on the floor next to the mattress.

I entered with an armload of clean clothes and let them cascade down to the mattress. I turned the lamp on, the 15-watt bulb strained to come to life. I flopped on the mattress and lay there motionless for a few moments, waiting for the dizziness, like a slow moving train, to pass.

Once the caboose moved on I rose and removed the worn out duct tape from my shoe. I dug into one of the boxes and pulled out a dwindling roll of silver duct tape. I re-wrapped the shoe with my foot still in it. Experience had taught that if you don't keep your foot in the shoe, you end up wrapping the duct tape too tight.

Mary came in and sat cross-legged on the mattress and started folding clothes. She silently watched me finish taping my shoe. When I put the roll of duct tape back in its box she took a pair of my underpants and placed them over my head.

"I'm not an animal," I Merricked. "I'm a human being."

Mary laughed and pulled the underpants from my head. I took them and folded them in half.

"I was thinking about going to see your dad on one of my days off," she said.

I grunted an acknowledgement. I folded a stripped tee.

"Would you like to do that?" she asked. "Would you like to see your dad?"

I shrugged.

We finished folding. I put my pile into one of the boxes. Mary gathered up her things.

"Well get some rest," she said.

She left and closed the door.

I undressed down to my underpants. From under my pillow I pulled out an adult's aging and threadbare olive drab tee shirt that I slept in. I slipped it over my head.

I had made my bed that morning. I didn't always do that. Sometimes I liked crawling under jumbled covers even if it meant my feet stuck out. Sometimes I would make the bed. But what I liked best was when Mom would make the bed with me in it. After the bottom sheet was on and the pillow cased, I would climb in. Then she would put the top sheet on (sometimes over my head) and tuck it in. Then she'd place the quilt her grandmother made for her over the sheet. It felt like perfection. I haven't thought about this in years.

I slid under the covers. I turned out the light. I lay there in the dark. I was ambivalent about seeing my dad. "Would you like to see your dad?" was not real to me. It was just a string of words.

It felt like the room was spinning ever so slightly like a drowsy carousel; maybe it was the nicotine. I'm not sure. Maybe it was time steadily winding down and I could feel it even then. There were nine days left.

Sunday, August 30

I awoke the next morning to a rhythmic 'tink' of spoon to bowl. I crawled off the mattress and went to the kitchen. There I found Alex standing over the sink slurping up a bowl of cereal. Alex was probably in his forties, it's hard to tell when you're seven going on eight. He was short, dark and wiry, and he was missing most of his front teeth. When Alex was lost in thought his tongue would explore the vast area of his mouth where teeth had once been. He wore only a pair of jeans while he leaned against the counter, one bare foot crossed over the other.

"Hey," I said.

"Hey," he slurped.

Alex was the current occupant of the other upstairs room. Alex was homosexual, I know because he told me. Heck he told everybody. He'd say he was "homosexual"--that's the term he used, I suppose he never took to "gay." I didn't know what homosexual meant and the only one who seemed to care that he was one was Alex. Looking back on it Alex was the most un-gay looking gay man I ever met. No flair, no style, no teeth. He was too skinny and sometimes he'd get the shakes. Alex was a roofer when he worked. I don't know how he could do it and still be so skinny, but he did.

"Is the Crazy Lady out there again?" Alex asked.

I turned and looked through the front window. The Crazy Lady was out at the mailboxes, going from box to box and looking inside. I guess Sunday to her meant the mail would be coming nine or ten times, just like any other day.

"Yeah," I delivered.

"Someone should call the cops," Alex said. But we didn't call the cops. No one did. Ever.

Alex slurped a bit more cereal.

"Where's Uncle Henry?" I asked.

"Attic. Hungry?"

"I guess. Is that Cheerios?"

"Mmm, hmm. But we're out of milk."

"What'd you pour on it?"

"Brandy."

That explained the shakes. Something else about Alex, this guy had no navel. I'm serious, no navel, just all smooth. It made me think of an old Star Trek rerun. William Shatner was stripped to the waist and fighting some alien and Shatner had no nipples! Just smooth skin where nipples should be. I later wondered why no one ever asked him about it.

"So Bill, what happened to your nipples?" Jay Leno would ask while he was hosting The Tonight Show.

"Just never had any," William Shatner would reply.

"Really?!" Jay Leno astounds.

"Well, I don't think I would have used them for anything. However," William Shatner would go on, "and this is a little known fact, I was the actual chest model for the 'Ken' doll."

"That's amazing."

"I don't know who the poor sap was who modeled for hips and thighs."

Alex took another bite of brandied Cheerios. "Why don't you have a belly button?" I asked.

"Hernia."

That made sense.

"Did it hurt?" I asked. "When the hernia got your belly button?"

"Yeah, I guess."

"Thought so. I saw 'em on TV once--a whole pack of 'em chasing a zebra."

Alex laughed so hard brandy leaked from his eyes. Through the laughing he said something I interpreted to be:

"A pack of hernias? Oh man. Yeah it hurt when they bit it off."

"What's so funny?"

The attic was accessed through a half door in the wall in Henry's bedroom. The door was about five feet up and Henry kept a chair in front of it to use as a stepladder to enter the attic. When I climbed on the chair the bottom of the door was just below my shoulders. I put my hands at the bottom and jumped up to my waist, then lifted my knee to the threshold. I scooted in.

The attic spanned the length of the house. It wasn't dark and scary like television attics. It had windows at both ends that didn't open. The attic smelled like it still had its original air, trapped there for seven decades, and mixed with the exhales of past denizens; it smelled like history. Two bare light bulbs hung in the middle of the room about eight feet apart, 'though only one was lit. The floor was finished so one could walk freely about, but only if one were about four feet tall. The exposed roof beams met at the peak about seven feet up from the floor and angled down to three feet on one side and down to nothing on the other. The attic was crammed with boxes of various sizes filled with precious objects, heirlooms, junk and dreams. There was an old couch needing to be re-stuffed and re-covered, some floor lamps needing re-wiring, a tricycle needing to be repainted and needing a toddler, a queen size bed frame needing a bed, some buckets needing to be put to work, and a pile of clothes needing time to come back in style. There was even a spare tire mounted on a rusting light green rim needing a whole car.

Henry was busy moving boxes around like a 15 Tile Puzzle. He selected one and opened it. Henry was long-haired and always looked like he had two weeks worth of beard growing. I'd never seen him shave nor seen him clean-shaven. He just always had two weeks worth of beard, like he was born with two weeks worth and would be buried with two weeks worth.

Henry was my dad's older brother. He was a relic of a commune hippy--eternally dusty with a firm belief of utopia found in sharing possessions and marijuana. He grew his own in a small patch near the river; the exact location he kept to himself. He used some fifty-year-old chicken shit as fertilizer. Henry was a big believer in fifty-year-old chicken shit.

"Hey little man," Henry said looking over to me.

"What're you looking for?" I asked.

"My youth, small fry, my youth."

"It's in one of these boxes?"

"I'm pretty sure that's where I left it." Henry said as he stood and wiped his hands on his jeans.

"Can I help?" I asked.

"Sure."

"What's it look like?"

"Big, black and rubber."

So we looked through boxes trying to find Uncle Henry's youth.

❊ ❊ ❊

The day was moving on and so was our progress searching through boxes. I finished with the one I was looking in and moved it aside. Behind it was an old metal-framed footlocker looking like Pandora's temptation.

"What about this one?" I asked.

"That one's yours."

"Mine?"

"Sort of. Your dad's stuff is in it. The footlocker is ancient. My dad, your granddad, used it during dubbya dubbya dos."

I looked at the footlocker. Henry opened another box and launched into a monologue. I know I didn't really pay attention to him at the time, but because of the events it preceded I can remember every word he said while I explored the footlocker like he'd typed them directly on my cerebral cortex. I pulled over the box I'd just finished with, sat down on it and creaked open the footlocker.

"Yeah Frank," Henry said, "your ol' dad, well he gets his draft notice just after the government says the last US combat troops have pulled out of Viet Nam, which leads to a landslide victory for ol' Tricky Dick--McGovern didn't have a fuckin' chance."

Inside the footlocker was my dad's stuff. Old jeans, worn out tri-fold wallet--empty, high school yearbook from his junior year....

"Frank takes that draft notice," Henry continued, his nose buried in a box, "and decides to join the Marines since there is no more fighting in Viet Nam and he figures being a 'jarhead' will look good on his resume. Your ol' man's in San Diego when Kissinger announces 'peace is at hand.'"

..there were tee shirts in the footlocker that matched the one I slept in, khaki socks and under shorts, khaki belt, empty ammo pouch that once held twenty rounds of M-16 ammo, two-quart nylon canteen with shoulder strap, which I slipped over my shoulder, jungle hat known as a "boonie", which I slipped onto my head, and...a box of cigars.

"Ugh." I grunted. I got queasy just looking at the cigar box.

"After boot camp he comes home and marries your mom on Christmas day and two weeks later don't you know they ship his ass off to Viet Nam," Henry droned on.

I was born while my dad was in Viet Nam. I wondered about the cigars, had they been in celebration? I went back into the footlocker and while moving some shirts I felt something. I pulled out a small jewelry case. I carefully opened it. It held a Purple Heart.

"Then...after Nixon's peace with fuckin' honor speech...on January twenty-seventh nineteen hundred and seventy-three... Frank gets wounded."

I gingerly lifted the gleaming medal. The obverse was a profile of George Washington, like a gold quarter for the wounded. The reverse formed a raised heart and the words FOR MILITARY MERIT in all capital letters. It sparkled like pain.

"He never would say where, An Loc probably--at least that's what the 'govmint' would cop to. I wouldn't be surprised if he was in Cambodia or Laos or...Eureka!" Henry said.

I looked behind me at Henry. He pulled an old torn wetsuit from a box. I replaced the medal and closed the footlocker. I stood and went over to Henry and the wetsuit.

"Is that it?" I asked.

"Yep."

"Your youth is covered with dust," I said.

"More than you know, little man."

Henry 15 puzzled the boxes back into an order known only to him. He placed the box containing his youth in front of the open door and with me still wearing the boonie and canteen we retreated with honor from the attic.

Down in the kitchen Henry set the box holding his youth on the table. Inside the box were two wetsuits. He took one out as Alex and I watched. The wetsuit was stiff and had numerous tears.

"We can rebuild it," Henry said running water into the sink. "We have the technology."

So we embarked on a mission to repair Henry's youth.

Henry pushed the torn wetsuit into the clear water of the now full sink. The sink water turned gray with dust and old memories of sea salt as Henry pushed, pulled and kneaded the black rubber suit.

Alex hung the now clean wetsuit to dry over the top of the back door while Henry drowned the other wetsuit. Once sufficiently satisfied with the cleanliness of the wetsuit, Henry took a chair from around the dining table and placed it on the back step. He hung the second wetsuit over the back of the chair.

Alex polished off the last of the brandy and chased it down with an Olympia beer. Henry extracted a beer for himself from the refrigerator. He yanked off the pull-tab, dropped it down the opening of the can and took a long swig. Myself, I did the same with a can of cola. I had to hold the cold can between my knees to get the leverage needed to wrench the pull-tab off.

Henry rifled through the "junk" drawer in the kitchen and targeted a bottle of rubber cement. I had used the same rubber cement a few weeks earlier to make fake "boogers" that I strategically placed throughout the house. No one ever mentioned them and one day I noticed they were gone. The best laid plans of mice and seven-year-olds....

Henry took the first wetsuit down and applied rubber cement to one of its tears. He held the glued pieces together for a minute then went to work on the next tear.

Alex slipped the hood of the wetsuit on over his head and downed the last of his beer. He looked like a toothless sea lion.

I applied rubber cement to a tear while Henry supervised. The rubber cement smelled sweet. "Careful not too breathe too deep," Henry said, "that stuff'll glue your brain."

"What if your brain's got a rip?" I asked.

"Tell him, Alex."

"Can't," Alex said. "My brain's both ripped and glued."

"Let that be a lesson," Henry said.

We finally finished and left the repaired wetsuits hanging out back to cure.

Broken Record

* * *

I wore the boonie; it's shadow hiding my eyes. I'd filled the canteen and had it draped over my shoulder and across my chest. I wandered the side of the highway spending the summer's Sunday afternoon the best possible way, with nothing to do.

Up ahead was a roadside display of Mexican imports with a hand painted sign reading "Mexican Imports" in red letters on a field of white. Next to the Mexican imports was a small shack that housed a palm reader. There was also a sign that said "Palm Reading" that had an upraised hand and an all-seeing eye in the center of the palm. On the shack's covered porch was a large glass container of tea, steeping in the sun.

I stopped to look at the Mexican imports. There were birdbaths with "Winged Victory" as their pedestal. There were Statues of Liberty, but they didn't look quite right; something about the face was off but I wasn't sure what and I was unable to perform a side-by-side comparison. There were planters of all sorts and dog figurines to guard your fireplace. There were ceramics in red and gray and white. Overseeing all of this was a hefty man wearing Bermuda shorts and flattened flip-flops. The size of his enormous tank top tee shirt had so many "X"s in front of the "L" that it was pornographic. His dark shoulders had baked well under the summer sun, but when he lifted his slab-like arm to wipe sweat from his forehead his underarms were as white as a shark's belly.

The palm reader came out and poured some tea over a glass of ice. I watched her from the shade of my boonie. She spotted me.

"You want your palm read?" she smiled.

"I don't know," I said.

She wasn't what I expected. I thought she'd be old and tired, worn from years of seeing the hell in people and their lives. But she was young, maybe the same age as Mary. She wore a cloth loosely wrapped around her body that allowed her breasts to flow as she bent and poured tea into her glass. She wore a second cloth wrapped as a skirt that showed her ankles and bare feet. Her eyes were as dark as her hair, like night dreaming of black pearls.

"Hold up your hand," she said.

I held up my hand, palm facing her.

"It's cone-shaped. You know what that means?"

I knew what "cone-shaped" was but I didn't think that was what she meant.

"No," I said. "What does it mean?"

"You should let me read your palm. Do you want to know your future?"

"Can you really tell the future?" I asked.

"For five dollars I can. Don't you think your future is worth five dollars?"

I don't know how much I thought it was worth then. I know now it wasn't worth five dollars and maybe knowing then would have been priceless.

"I don't have five dollars," I said.

"How about two dollars?" the palm reader said. "For two dollars I'll read two lines, maybe your head and life lines, or your fate and love lines. Don't you want to know about your love line?"

"I don't have two dollars. I don't have any money," I said.

"I'm so sorry."

"It's all right," I said. "What about you?"

"What about me?"

"Can you read your own palm?"

"Yes, I've read my own palm."

"What did it say?" I asked.

"It said I would meet a young man."

"Was that me?" I asked.

"Maybe," she said.

"Did it say that I wouldn't have any money?"

"Well," she said, "there's broke and there's broke. D'you know what I mean?"

"Yeah, Mary says that," I said. "She says there's broke like we don't have enough to pay the PG&E and there's broke like we don't have any money at all."

"Who's Mary?"

"My mom."

"Ahh. Well I guess I thought my palm said PG&E broke."

"You might want to try washing your hands," I said. "I know that when I wash my hands sometimes they look completely different."

"They're clean," she said showing me both the front and back of her hands. "Perhaps I should dirty them up a bit."

"Maybe."

She smiled at me; a small sweet smile like summer dessert. Her smile faded to an expressionless void. She looked sad. Did she know my future? She turned with her tea and dissolved into the house.

I'm not sure if I actually saw her smile fade. I'm not sure if I actually saw her turn and evanesce. It feels like I did. It feels like I should have. Maybe my memory is so desperate to find meaning that it wanted the palm reader to know my future--at least my immediate future--and to know that I was just five dollars from changing it.

There's broke and there's broke...and then there's broke.

* * *

Wayne and I walked in crouched reconnaissance looking for "Charlie". The woods were thick with the smell of "VC". My M-16 rifle was camouflaged as a small branch. Wayne had an unloaded bb gun.

We spotted an enemy squirrel at the base of a tree. Suddenly gunfire erupted shattering the silence and sounding freakishly like two boys' voices mimicking machine gun fire. Wayne chose the time honored "UH" sound from the back of the throat while I preferred the "TH" sound made by pressing the tongue against the back of the teeth and forcing air through them. "UH, uh, uh, uh, uh, uh, uh, uh, uh, uh, uh, uh!!!" "TH, th, th, th, th, th, th, th, th, th, th, th, th, th!!!" The squirrel scampered up the tree.

Later I hid in a tree. Wayne walked slowly underneath looking for the enemy--me.

I dropped from the tree behind Wayne firing away. "TH, th, th, th, th, th, th, th!"

Wayne did the dance of a hundred bullets, then crumpled to the ground.

I, now his war buddy, rushed to his side.

"Hold on man," I said, "you're going to be all right."

"I'm cold."

Wayne coughed up invisible blood. His eyes rolled over white. I took the cap off the canteen. I lifted Wayne's head and gave him a sip of water.

"Just hold on," I said.

"Tell...tell Jane I love her."

I let Wayne's head drop to the ground.

"Who's Jane?"

"Oh c'mon," Wayne said. "Nobody."

That was what death was in the summer of 1981.

My God how naïve we were. The thing about being naïve is that at the time you don't feel it. You mostly don't even know it. You don't know what you don't know and you don't much think about it. But once naïveté is lost you can never regain it. In eight days my naïveté would bleed out and I would never be the same. Once you know something...

We sat with our backs resting against a tree. Wayne pulled a pack of Belairs from his pocket and flipped out a cigarette. He had a book of matches slipped inside the Belairs' cellophane skin, which he slid out, lit one and set the cigarette ablaze.

Wayne offered me a drag but I just shook my head no. I offered Wayne a swig from the canteen. He accepted and took a drink.

I stared off into the distance.

"Who's Jane?"

Wayne punched me in the shoulder as I laughed.

Monday, August 31

At dawn the next morning we loaded into Henry's early 50's Dodge pick-up and headed out to the coast with Henry's youth in search of abalone.

I climbed into the bed of the pick-up and sat beside an aging red Coleman cooler. Next to the cooler was a box that held the repaired wetsuits, some towels and some potato chips. Next to the box was a dark blue sleeping bag. I wrapped myself in the sleeping bag then fixed the chinstrap of the boonie up under my chin.

Alex, riding shotgun, closed the passenger door, while Henry stepped on the starter. Mary, wedged in between them, turned to smile at me through the back window. The Dodge pulled away.

Henry had to double-clutch the old Dodge to shift gears. I heard the engine wind up, felt Henry disengage the clutch and shift from low to neutral, engage the clutch, rev the engine, press down on the clutch again and slip the lever into second. The truck picked up speed. We headed west.

Highway 12 unwound under us as we made our way through the coastal hills. We were making for Highway 1 just between Bodega Bay and Jenner, where we would then head north toward Fort Ross. Henry knew a spot where, he said, great herds of abalone once roamed like undersea buffalo. He smiled when he said it.

The old Dodge curved through hills where apple orchards and vineyards competed for land. The apples were Gravenstein, a very tart variety that made excellent pies. When they're ripe Gravensteins have a yellowish-green skin with red spots and streaks. I don't know what kind of grapes hung from the uniform rows of vines that covered the hills like corduroy.

I liked how you could smell the ocean before finally being able to see it. It was like a promise from God. A scent of timeless grace embracing the hills and highway. It smelled like fun, it smelled carefree, it smelled like summer.

The tree-covered hills gave way to bleak treeless coastal ranges where Highway 12 poured into Highway 1. I could smell the saltwater. I filled my lungs with anticipation. I turned around and knelt in the bed of the truck and gazed through the windshield between Mary and Alex. We rounded a bend and there was the Pacific Ocean stretching like a lazy cat all the way to the end of the world.

We headed north up the coast highway winding our way over cliffs and through gullies. Henry constantly geared down to second or geared up to third in an effort to keep the flathead six-cylinder engine at the right speed.

I turned back and watched the road spool out from under the pick-up. There was an occasional house that would pass by and shrink away. We went through a small town and as we were leaving I saw a sign that told me the town was Jenner. "Welcome to Jenner" the sign said as we left.

After awhile Henry pulled left across the highway and stopped at a small bluff on the side of the road. He turned the ignition key off and the engine sputtered and spit until it finally gave up. I was up and over the side of the truck as the engine wheezed out its last breath.

There was a small footpath through the blackberries, coastal brush lupine, huckleberries and poison oak that led down a treacherous bluff and out to the sand and ocean.

Henry and Alex both stripped down to nothing and while stark naked poured cornstarch into their wetsuits to aid with putting them on. They sprinkled cornstarch on themselves and slipped dusted legs into dusted wetsuits.

Mary placed the box holding the towels and chips on the cooler and she and I carried the cooler down the footpath and out to the beach. Mary used one hand for the cooler and carried the sleeping bag with the other. I struggled using both hands for the cooler. We both wore cutoff jeans; Mom wore a halter-top tied in a simple square knot behind her back.

Mom and I set up camp--meaning we laid out the towels and set the cooler, box and sleeping bag nearby--while Henry and Alex made their way down the path through the brush.

Henry and Alex trudged down the beach to the rocky shore wearing their black rubber wetsuits. They looked like shadows. I noticed then that Alex's wetsuit was made for a woman. He smiled a big gummy smile as he pressed in the molded mounds formed on the chest.

Henry carried a rubber inner tube with a piece of canvas

stretched across one side--it was a float to hold the abalone. In the float were a couple of diving masks, snorkels, pry-bars and measuring tools.

With tennis shoes covering their rubber booties, Henry and Alex entered the water to crawl over submerged rocks hunting for abalone.

After laying out the towels, I headed down to the wet sand and jumped and played in the surf. Mary followed and stood nearby, standing ankle deep in the surging water.

Mary watched Henry surface with an abalone.

"Jimmy," she said. "Look."

I looked over to where she was pointing and saw Henry use his measuring iron to check the size of what looked to be a rock. He put the rock in the float.

"Why is he getting rocks?" I asked.

"It's not a rock, that's an abalone."

"Is that where bologna sandwiches come from?"

"No. Aaaaabalone is a mussel, like oysters. Bologna comes from the deli."

I thought about muscles and sandwiches.

"Looks like a rock," I said.

Mary smiled. She turned to the dry sandy beach. She shielded her eyes to the morning sun as she slowly walked back to camp. Mary untied the back of her halter and lay face down on a towel on the sand.

The beach held great possibilities of exploration and discovery. I spotted a small crab on the wet sand. Being careful of its pinchers, I found a twig that I used to try get the crab to clamp on. No luck. I used the twig to hustle the crab back to sea.

I watched a tide pool. There were animals that looked like strange underwater plants. There were creatures that moved about by curling their bodies this way and that. There was a small orange starfish clinging to a rock. I touched an anemone with the twig.

I found a piece of driftwood and used it as a walking stick as I trudged along the shore. I walked until Henry and Alex were just bobbing black blobs that floated on the water and from time to time disappeared underneath. I couldn't see Mary at all.

I rounded a large rock and saw a very small baby seal on the dry sand of the beach. The seal barked a nervous cry. I hunkered down and watched. I took a few duck steps closer. The seal cried out again. I took the walking stick and gently stroked the seal's back with it.

"There, there now." I said. "It's okay. No one's going to hurt you."

The seal began to calm down. It smelled like wet dog.

"There, there. There, there."

A wave broke and ran up the beach near the seal. I used the stick to gently prod the seal closer to the surf. It scooted a bit and stopped. I prodded a little more and the seal moved closer to the breaking waves. Water rushed over the seal. The wave pulled the seal closer down the shore. The seal made its way further down the wet sand. Another wave rushed in and the seal swam away. I walked slowly back along the shore.

That's the way it should have happened.

In reality the baby seal was dead. I just didn't know it. I guess I thought it was too scared to move so I used the stick to push it down the beach until a wave claimed it. It was years later when

I realized that the seal was dead. Once you know something you can never un-know it and it seems like you've always known it. And I feel like I'd always known the seal was dead and that I should have done something...

Using the stick I wrote my name in the wet sand along the shore. Capital "J", small "i", capital "M", capital "M", capital "Y".

I didn't really know about burials then, 'though it feels like I did. I had seen them on TV; Popeye would punch Bluto and Bluto would skid along the ground building up a mound of dirt and when he stopped skidding he was under the dirt beneath a cartoon headstone. Of course Bluto would be in the very next scene.

I threw the stick out to sea.

I still feel guilty that I didn't give that baby seal a proper burial.

The sun had begun its gradual descent where it would extinguish itself in the calm waves of the Pacific Ocean.

When I got back to camp Mary had a fire going and hotdogs roasting on sticks. Henry and Alex had their wetsuits unzipped and pulled down to their waists. Alex gummed into a hotdog. I looked into the cooler at the day's catch: four abalone. Alex told of fantastic adventures diving for abalone (this was his first time) using excited eyes and big gestures. With a full mouth and no teeth, I didn't understand a word he said. But his gestures and sparkle told me the whole story in great detail.

From sweat and starch, Henry and Alex smelled like cornbread. Now all these years later...when I smell cornbread, I think of the beach and abalone.

The sun was gone and had been replaced by a cool breeze. I wrapped a towel around my shoulders. Henry sipped an RC Cola.

Mom had a cola too, but she just held it. Her eyes stared down the shoreline, but her thoughts were on holiday.

Alex had trudged back to the pick-up and returned with an old cigar box. He flopped cross-legged on the sand and opened the box. Inside were marijuana and Zig Zag papers and things.

By the light of the fire, Alex, cigar box in his lap, tried to roll a joint. His hands shook, probably from lack of alcohol. Henry and I watched. Alex spilled some weed on the sand.

"Careful with that." Henry said. "That's good stuff. I grew it in fifty-year-old chicken shit. It's as strong as a hundred camels in the court yard."

Alex tried again, but continued to struggle.

Mary looked over at me. The light from the fire cast a glimmer upon her face like sunset. She was as beautiful then as she would ever wish to be.

"Here, let me," I said to Alex.

I took the cigar box and joint from Alex. From the box I took a small hand roller. I emptied the marijuana from the joint into the roller and added a bit more from the cigar box. I pressed the rollers together and rolled them tight. I took a new paper and inserted it into the roller. I rolled to the gum line, then licked the gum and spun it through. I opened the roller and took out the joint and gave it to Alex.

Alex twisted the ends tight.

"Thanks man," Alex said.

Alex struck a match and lit the joint.

I dozed in half-sleep on Mary's lap, my head resting against her shoulder, while Henry drove us home. Alex sat between Mary and Henry. Night had painted the world black and gray. The weak headlights of Henry's pickup only imagined they lit up the road.

The Dodge pulled up to the small house. Henry cut the ignition and set the brake.

"Jimmy," Mom said, "wake up. We're here."

I woke up saying, "I'm awake."

Mary opened the door and we climbed out. I groggled to the back of the truck and dreamt that I started to unload stuff. Mom stopped me.

"You go on to bed," she said, "we'll get this."

I didn't argue.

I stumbled into the house and found my room. I felt like I could sleep for days. But I didn't.

Sleep was as evasive as contentment. I tossed in the bed. I tried lying still for a bit, but failed. I just couldn't sleep. I felt melancholy. Maybe it was the baby seal weighing even then like a lead apron of guilt. Maybe it was the fates silently telling me that time was running out and there were only seven days left. Maybe it was just being awakened from the drive and having to make my way into bed. My mom used to carry me to bed and I was barely aware of it as I slept on her shoulder. So even after time had gone to bed and was snoring I got up.

In the living room Mary slept in the hide-a-bed. I looked through the soft focus of tired eyes and watched her sleep.

"Mom?"

"What is it, honey?"

"I can't remember the last time you carried me to bed."

"Well it's been over thirty years."

"I know," I said, "I guess I wished I had remembered better. If I knew it was going to be the last time, I would have tried to remember better."

"Life is full of those moments," she said. "The last time we climb a tree, the last time we see someone, our last first kiss. It's a series of 'last times' that we usually don't remember."

"But we should."

"We should," Mary said, "but we don't...because mostly we don't think it will be the last time."

Mom made room for me in the hide-a-bed and I climbed in under the covers. We lay there like spoons in a drawer. It was quiet.

"I think this was the last time this happened," I said.

"I think you're right. But you didn't wake me up then."

"I know," I whispered. "Good night mom."

She didn't answer. Her breathing was soft and regular. She was asleep. She was always asleep.

Tuesday, September 1

Henry was already up when I awoke. I found him out on the back step with the cooler of abalone. He had one out and was working to separate the muscle from the shell using an abalone iron. The iron looked like an ice cream scoop that had been run over by a steamroller.

I looked in the cooler. One abalone was stuck to the side of the cooler; another abalone was stuck to the first. The third looked like it was coming out of its shell. I closed the cooler and sat on it.

"One's trying to get out of its shell," I said.

"It's relaxed," Henry said.

"Oh."

Henry cut the muscle attachment releasing the abalone from its shell. The freed abalone looked gross, all guts and slime. My lip curled and my left eye squinted.

"Don't look too appetizing, does it," Henry said catching my look.

"Nope."

"This one's female."

"How can you tell?" I asked.

"See this?" Henry said pointing to a greenish lump curling around the side of the abalone. "It's the gonads, the sex organ. In a male it's a cream color."

"Oh." I pondered this for a while. Henry grabbed up a sharp knife.

"But if they're inside the shell, how does the boy abalone tell it's a girl abalone?" I asked.

"They don't worry about it."

"Do you cook the gonads?"

"No," Henry said as he skillfully cut away the guts and gonads. "We just cook the muscle. So all this stuff," he said pointing with the blade of the knife, "heart, guts, eyes, mouth gets cut away." He continued slicing.

"The thing has eyes?"

"Not anymore," Henry said. "I then cut away this stuff," he continued as he sliced off the black tentacled epipodium, "but I can't remember what it's called. I also cut off this part, which is the bottom of the foot."

Henry finished cutting and was left with one cleaned abalone.

"Then what?" I asked.

"Then I slice it into steaks, beat the shit out of it and then fry it up."

"Why do you beat the shit out of it?"

"To tenderize it," he said. "I'll show you."

Henry sliced a steak from the freshly cleaned abalone and laid it on the concrete step. He grabbed a heavy wooden mallet that looked like it had been made by a Neanderthal thirty thousand years ago and began whacking the steak.

"Can I try?" I asked.

Henry gave me the mallet and I was gainfully employed for the next hour and a half. Henry cleaned the abalone and I beat the shit out of 'em.

After we cleaned the abalone and had beaten the steaks into submission, Henry fried up some for lunch. He cracked open a half a dozen eggs using only one hand to break them apart and whisked them up in a mixing bowl. He sprinkled in a bunch of spices all the while saying "a little of this, a little of that, a pinch of this, some of that, but none of the other, definitely none of the other." He crunched in a handful of soda crackers and mixed everything together. He dipped in the abalone steaks and spread them out in a large blackened iron skillet filled with hot grease.

The smell brought Mary in from the living room. She was wrapped in a blanket. Her eyes were closed; she looked like she was a certified somnambulist. She pulled a cola from the refrigerator, pulled the tab and sat at the table all while possibly still asleep. She balled her hands into fists, setting the left fist on the table, the right fist on the left and her chin on the right. She squinted her eyes open then closed them again.

Alex dropped in from upstairs. His hair was slick after showering.

"Catch 'em and eat 'em, that's what I say," Alex said.

Alex grabbed a beer from the fridge and cracked it open. He drank long.

I got some bread plates from the cabinet. I went to the flatware drawer and took out four forks. "Do we need knives?" I asked.

"We shouldn't," Henry said. "Not after the beating you dished out."

Henry filled the plates and we dined alfresco on fried abalone steak.

❊ ❊ ❊

A twig snapped under my foot. I stopped and held my breath. I listened for snipers. I could hear the rumble of a diesel engine thundering nearby. I continued scouting the woods trying to spot the Ho Chi Minh trail, just in case Wayne and I resumed hostilities. We never did.

I climbed up a tree. Just beyond the woods was a small cemetery. In the cemetery a worker in a backhoe was digging a grave. The backhoe looked like a giant scorpion. It stuck its stinger into the earth and pulled out a bucket load of dirt.

When he finished the backhoe operator backed up his equipment a few feet from the grave. Another worker began to cover the mound of excavated dirt with rolls of bright green Astro-turf.

I selected a good branch then hung upside down by my knees. I was now Australian. Upside down the backhoe operator joined the other worker and helped cover the dirt.

It's funny how we decide to dig a big hole to bury our dead and have for thousands of years, yet in these days the sight of the mound of dirt so offends our fragile sensibilities that we resort to covering it with Astro-turf.

An upside down black Cadillac hearse slowly drove into the cemetery, two upside down cars followed. Seeing the hearse sparked a memory of the last time I saw Hahnteehurth.

I don't even know if it's Hahnteehurth or Hahntee Hurth or maybe Han T. Herth. All I know is that everyone called him

Hahnteehurth and that's how I picture it. Hahnteehurth knew my father in the service and lived in the basement of Penngrove House when Mary and I stayed there for a few months. Like Hahnteehurth, we lived in the basement. When we were there it was called Penngrove Three.

Penngrove One had been a commune formed by school bus hippies trying to build their own Merry Prankster utopia at the dawning of the age of Aquarius. Penngrove Two housed east coast whiz kids who were on the leading edge of personal computing and video game consoles. Penngrove Three was the home of starving artists, with anything and everything their canvas.

Hahnteehurth was a junk artist. I remember watching him take a broken wall clock and turn it into art. He completely disassembled the clock where it became a pile of gears, springs, supports and connectors. Then he painted each piece a different fluorescent color. After the pieces had dried, Hahnteehurth glued or soldered them together so that every piece was near its proper spot but still visible. He then mounted it on the wall and called it "Unsprung."

Hahnteehurth worked from time to time making sandwiches at the café in Muir Woods National Park. One night he came home with several long ham tins and an idea. The tins were four inch square and longer than my arm. I helped Hahnteehurth wash out the tins while he told me his idea--he was going to make ashtrays, big deep ashtrays that would take forever to fill up so people wouldn't have to empty them all the time, and when they got full you could just throw them out.

The tins had been opened with a standard can opener to remove the ham, but Hahnteehurth had saved the tops. Using a hammer and nail, he pounded holes in the center of the tops. He cut slits into the rim on the middle of each of the four sides. He then took the tops and turned them one quarter turn so they looked like diamonds over squares, he wedged the tips of the diamonds into the slits. He bent the tips down, securing the tops in place. The tops would then hold a cigarette, had holes for the ash to fall through and at each corner there was an opening to drop the snuffed out cigarette butt. It worked and was useful.

But then Hahnteehurth decided he had to decorate the tins. "Wouldn't be right to advertise canned ham in everyone's living room," he said. And so he did, decorating the tins with tapes and yarns and glues and leathers and shiny stones. They were beautiful and no one ever threw them out. Most people wouldn't even use them as ashtrays.

While we were still at Penngrove House, Hahnteehurth had been injured in a car wreck where a military buddy of his had died. I wasn't aware of what had happened then, but time and experience sometimes fill gaps in your knowledge. The last time I saw Hahnteehurth he'd shown up in the basement of Penngrove House bruised, gaunt and supported by wooden crutches. Mary helped him gather up some of his things; I did too. We took them out to a car he had borrowed from a friend. It was a black 1951 Chevy panel wagon. We loaded his stuff in the back; then Mary gave him a long hug. Hahnteehurth awkwardly maneuvered himself behind the wheel of the long black wagon and propped his crutches in the passenger seat. On the seat in the shadow of the crutches was a US flag folded in a triangle. He drove away pushed by a cloud of smoke and dust. I never saw, nor heard of Hahnteehurth again.

The memory of that black Chevy driving away lasted only an instant hanging underneath that branch. It took far less time than telling it, but it has lingered there, upside down, for years. Unsprung.

❃ ❃ ❃

I rode my bike along a deserted rural two-lane highway. I slowed to a stop and got off the bike.

An electrical wire spanned the width of the street and draped across it was a ratty pair of sneakers. A rock flew and hit one of the sneakers. That was me; I did that.

I hurled another rock at the sneakers but missed. I searched the ground for more rocks. I gathered up two and threw again. The first rock missed, but the second found its mark causing the sneaker to swing on the wire. I tossed another rock.

Time had tromped on and my arm was growing sore and tired. I picked up another rock.

Shadows were lengthening. A rock sailed past the sneakers followed by another in rapid succession. Two other boys had joined me, both of whom threw rocks at the sneakers.

A rock hit the further shoe and it swung out, causing the near shoe to slip closer to the wire. We let loose a cheer in celebration of our progress.

One of the boys fired another rock. Our goal wasn't to just hit the sneakers; it was to knock them off the wire.

A baseball flew past the sneakers.

Now there were about a dozen boys, some as old as early teens, trying to knock the sneakers off the wire. A few other boys found positions down the street, baseball mitts in the ready to catch the misses. One of them snagged the miss and tossed the ball back to the crowd. Between them there were now three baseballs.

A new Chrysler approached from up the road. We all moved aside to let the car pass. We once again took aim.

Another miss.

A hit, but not hard enough to knock the sneakers down.

The sun was warm on our backs. A few more kids joined in, including Amy and Angie, identical twin blondes from my class, who stood straddling their identical bicycles. Although 'identical,' Amy was drawn, rail thin, maybe fifteen pounds lighter than her sister.

I threw a baseball and grazed one of the sneakers. I stepped aside.

One of the bigger boys took a try. His first throw flew wide and was caught by one of the boys down the street. He threw again and this time it flew true and hit its mark. The sneakers came down. Cheers rang out.

I gathered up the sneakers. They were Adidas.

One kid said, "Let's throw 'em back up there."

"Are you kidding?" another said. "It was too much work gettin' 'em down."

"I'll get rid of 'em." I offered.

The crowd disbursed--satisfied with their well-spent summer afternoon. I watched Amy and Angie ride off on their matching bikes. Angie waved. I waved back, the sneakers dangling by the laces that spanned my palm.

As I rode off down the street, my duct-taped sneakers swung

slightly on the wire. The Adidas were two sizes too big and I had to replace the laces. But truth be known, there's not much worse for a kid than having to wear shitty shoes.

❈ ❈ ❈

The sky began to darken as the day closed its eyes for the evening. I rode up to my house. I stopped and let the bike drop in the yard.

When I entered, the house was filled with about a dozen people. Two guys with electric guitars, Steve and Cap'n Anad, were trying to harmonize while strumming the Doobie Brothers' "Blackwater." Steve and the Cap'n were regulars at Henry's. The bass player, George, had been over occasionally during the time I lived at Uncle Henry's. A guy named John often brought over a full drum kit, but on this night he played bongos. John held a lit cigarette between his two front teeth while he rapped on the skins. Henry sat on the hide-a-bed with a woman snuggled up close to him. She was mid-thirties, long straight hair, maybe thirty pounds overweight, huge breasts. I caught Henry's eye.

"Mary still at work?" I hollered.

"I don't think she's off 'til after midnight," Henry yelled back.

I wandered to the kitchen.

In the kitchen some guy was cooking something on the stove. He was late-twenties, but very fair--he could've passed for fourteen. His eyes bugged out of their sockets like a Chihuahua and his hair hadn't seen shampoo since the previous decade and by the look of it would probably repel water.

I looked in the refrigerator. There wasn't much but beer and cola.

"Hey, grab me one of them beers" the guy said.

I took a beer out, wedged it between my knees, pulled the tab and I handed him the can.

"Thanks man," he said.

I extended my hand.

"I'm Jimmy," I said. "I live here."

The guy shook my hand.

"Dennis," he swallowed. "I live somewhere else."

"What're you making?"

"Rice."

"That's it?" I asked. "Just rice?"

"Just rice? Did I hear that right; just rice?"

Dennis picked me up and sat me on the counter. I guess he wanted to talk eye to eye.

"Rice is great," he continued. "It's nature's wonder food. There's about a billion uses for rice, man. You can eat it plain like this or with a fancy meal or with sushi. You can make rice flour or rice starch."

"Cereal. Like Rice Krispies," I threw in.

"Cereal right. You can make rice paste and rice paper. Umm rice oil." Dennis took a swig of beer. "Mmm. Beer, some beers are made with rice. Then there's rice wine and saké. In India, rice is associated with prosperity and with Lakshmi, the Hindu Goddess of Wealth."

"You know a lot about rice."

"Wait 'til we talk soy beans." Dennis lifted his beer in a toast then drank. I watched his Adam's apple bob.

Before and after. People often define and time their lives by either before or after events: "that was before Grandma died," "it was before graduation," "but that was just after the accident." I don't know if everyone does this; I certainly do. It seems like I always did, but I know I didn't before. Before and after. That's all there is. Talking to Dennis should be a memory lost among a hundred thousand memories but since it happened just before it feels like yesterday.

❋ ❋ ❋

When I was seven going on eight my Mom was working at the truck stop. I don't know if it had a real business name--everyone just called it the truck stop.

I rode my bike along the dark street past the Tropicana Cabanas; an old highway motel that was probably on its way to extinction even before the freeway bypassed it. Its palm tree-shaped sign at the end of the drive had faded like the dreams of motorists sleeping by the highway in the 1930's. All but a few of the neon tubes that outlined the letters and the palm fronds were broken or gone. What did survive was the overlapping 'yes' 'no' neon tubes that followed the word "Vacancy:" and on this night both were right.

There were no cabanas at the Tropicana Cabanas; it was one large building shaped like a huge letter "m" and sometime in the 60's the owner had converted it to apartments. Mary and I had lived there before moving in with Henry. We had a place on the middle leg of the "m" facing the pool. The pool was closed the entire time we lived there and the owner had strung chicken wire around it. The pool was solely for dead leaves, trash and rainwater, that had fermented into a black gooey tea. I didn't like the pool and stayed clear of it. I'd had a nightmare that I had fallen into the pool and was drowning in the 'Hoboke and Crocus.' That was what my sleeping brain called the black goo-tea. Hoboke and Crocus. Even now when I see a neglected fountain or a dying pool hosting dead leaves and rainwater, there'll be a sinister whisper: Hoboke and Crocus.

We didn't move because of the Hoboke and Crocus. We hadn't planned on moving at all. Mary liked the Tropicana Cabanas because it was close to the Truck Stop and she could walk to work when the weather was nice. Then one day the owner sent out eviction notices and began boarding up the vacant units. Within days graffiti went up and we went out, to Henry's.

I could see the sign out in front of the truck stop--Regular Unleaded 1.41 9/10. I parked my ride in front and dismounted. A few big rigs were parked nearby; one had its engine rumbling on idle. I entered the restaurant.

A trucker sat at one end of the counter downing an egg breakfast (served twenty-four hours). Another trucker slept in one of the booths. I could see Tom the cook under his paper hat, through the small window into the kitchen. He pulled an order ticket off the circular steel holder. Mary was talking to a woman sitting at the opposite end of the counter who was flirting with two guys sitting in a booth nearby. That was Sharon, the mother of a couple of my classmates, Angie and Amy. I've told you about them. Sharon was a friend of my mom's, not close, but they'd go out sometimes. Sharon was blond but she dyed her roots brown. She had broad shoulders and heavy breasts. Her chest narrowed at her waist then just kept narrowing to her hips and thighs. She was Y-shaped.

I took a stool at the middle of the counter. Mary spotted me, smiled and sidled over. She wore a black apron in which she kept her ticket book, a handful of pens and some paper napkins. She slid a menu in front of me.

"Hey trucker, rough day on the road?" she asked.

"That's a big 10-4. My arm is a little sore."

"How'd that happen?"

"Throwing rocks."

"I hope you didn't hurt anyone."

"Just an old pair of shoes."

"Well that's okay then. What can I do you for?" Mary asked.

"Can Tom make me a grilled cheese?"

"Fries?"

"How about rice?"

Mary smiled. "Rice?"

"Mmm hmm," I confirmed. "In India rice is a Goddess of some "P" word that I think means money. I figure we can use some of that."

"Yes we can. Rice it is."

Mary put the order in. I looked over to Sharon; she waved then returned to her flirting. Sharon always seemed to be with a different guy. Angie and Amy had more "uncles" than a lottery winner. Sharon never learned that sometimes nothing is better than something.

Mary "coffee'd" the trucker at the counter then rejoined Sharon. I slid off the stool and went around behind the counter. I took a glass and filled it with ice and cola. I placed it on the counter, grabbed a straw and retook my seat.

Tom brought out my sandwich and rice. Sharon had joined the two men. Mary stood with them talking and laughing. One of the men was short and soft. I could see his scalp through his hair. His hands were gentle and graceful; nails clean. He wore a tie. The other guy sat tall in the seat, both from height and from posture. His brown hair was parted in the middle and feathered over his ears. He wore motorcycle boots; the kind I heard Alex refer to as "shitkickers."

I bit into my grilled cheese sandwich.

Those two guys they're laughing with? Sharon could have her pick. Does she go for the short one with the paunch and thinning hair? The guy who has some junior–level management job at the poultry processing plant? Hell no, she chooses mister six foot four and exciting.

Are we just the sum of our choices?

I scooped some rice with my fork and looked back to Mary and Sharon. Sharon was smiling and happy as she moved closer to six four. Could she have possibly known where this would lead?

This is where: Six four beats the shit out of Sharon so bad that she looked like she was slammed through a hay baler then run over with it a couple of times just to be sure.

I finished my meal and said so long to Tom and Mary. I stepped outside like a long-haul trucker, mounted my rig and rode off. Dinner at the truck stop was six days before.

Sharon was in the hospital for weeks...she never regained the sight in her left eye. We didn't go to see her because that happened after.

Wednesday, September 2

I awoke to the sound of tinkering in the kitchen. I subtracted myself from my bed and unraveled my big tee shirt. I opened the door to my room and peered into the kitchen.

The woman Uncle Henry had been snuggling with the night before was busy quietly making eggs and potatoes for breakfast. She was clad only in light green panties that said 'Tuesday' on them. Her big breasts swayed as she worked. Her eyes were the same pale green as her underpants. The rest of the house was asleep.

"Smells good," I whispered.

She turned and smiled.

"You must be Jimmy," she said.

I nodded.

"I'm Linda," she introduced.

"Uncle Henry still sleeping?" I asked.

"Everyone is, 'cept you and me pal."

I looked into the living room. Mary slept in the hide-a-bed next to some unknown woman who was sleeping on top of the bedding wrapped in a quilt. Cap'n Anad snoozed in a chair. Dennis and some young girl are intertwined on the floor with blankets and pillows. I turned back to the kitchen.

"They almost never get up this early," I said. "I usually make cereal."

"Not today."

I sat at the small table and watched Linda cube potatoes.

"How come you're not still sleeping?" I asked.

"I had a dream. It woke me up and I couldn't go back to sleep."

"What was it about?"

"Had something to do with elephants."

"Elephants?" I asked. "What happened?"

"I'm not sure anymore. It was real vivid when I first got up but now I can't seem to remember."

"Dreams fade in the sunlight."

"Where did you hear that?" she asked.

"I don't remember," I said. I smiled, "Maybe I dreamed it."

Linda laughed and rubbed my head.

Once you know something you can never un-know it. I know that I had just met Linda on that soft summer morning, but it feels like I had always known her. Like she had always been Henry's girlfriend and always would be. Even though I know that's not true, it still feels true. I had just met her, yet she would be there. At the end of the day there would be but five days left and she would be there. I never told her what she meant to me. I'm not sure if I'm telling her now.

I quietly grabbed some silverware and set two places on the table. I then found a couple of mismatched plates and placed them on the table.

Linda had put the aluminum coffee pot on the stove and it had begun to percolate. The coffee pot was black from flame at its base and stained from coffee at the pour spout. I watched the brown liquid burble in the glass handle on the lid. Linda adjusted the flame under the coffee. I opened the refrigerator.

"No juice," I said. "Just Coke and beer."

"I'll just have coffee."

I closed the refrigerator.

"I'll have that too I guess."

I took a couple of matching Truck Stop coffee cups from the cupboard. I set them on the table then went to the pantry. I took out a container of Lady Lee instant chocolate mix and scooped a couple of spoonfuls into one of the coffee cups.

"You want some?" I asked.

Linda smiled. "No. I take mine black."

"It's really good," I tempted.

"Thanks all the same."

Linda turned the potatoes with a spatula. "Just about ready," she said. "I hope eggs and potatoes are okay? I couldn't find any bacon or sausage."

"Oh, I know," I excited.

I returned to the refrigerator and emerged with a foil wrapped package. I unwrapped the foil. Inside was leftover abalone.

"What is it?" Linda asked.

"Abalone," I replied. "It's good."

"If you say so."

Linda was skeptical but heated the abalone in a skillet. She poured in the beaten eggs and scrambled them with the abalone. Then she dished the scramble and potatoes on to the plates. I dug in while Linda set the pan on the stove and poured coffee in our cups. She placed my cup in front of me and sat down.

Linda tentatively tried a bite of scrambled eggs and abalone. She savored the flavor. "This is good," she said. "Where did you get it?"

"Henry got it out of the ocean," I answered, "it was gross 'til he cleaned it and I beat the shit out of it."

"I guess someone had too," she said.

I stirred my chocolate coffee and took a swig.

"Are you Henry's girlfriend?" I asked.

Linda smiled. "Don't know yet," she said. "We'll see. I just met him yesterday."

"He's nice. You'll like him."

We ate in silence for a short while. Then Linda said, "I know a joke about elephants. You wanna hear it?"

I nodded.

"Why do elephants wear red tennis shoes?" she asked. "Say why."

"Why?"

"To hide in cherry trees. You ever see an elephant in a cherry tree?"

"No," I said.

"See, it works."

I took another bite of breakfast. "That's a good one," I said.

❊ ❊ ❊

I had decided to perform some routine maintenance in my bike. This was the extent of my maintenance acumen: I balanced the bike upside down so that the handlebars and seat formed a tripod. With a small can of 3in1 oil I lubricated the chain at each sprocket. Then I turned the pedals as fast as I could, all the while keeping my left foot on the handlebars to keep the bike from toppling. So if you need your chain lubricated, I'm your guy.

I was in the process of turning the pedals when Wayne jogged up on a mission.

"Got a coffee can?" Wayne huffed.

"What?"

"Coffee can, big one, 'bout this big around." Wayne demonstrated the estimated circumference with his hands. I figured it to be about sixteen inches, but Wayne may have meant metric. I never asked him.

"I'll check," I said.

I went 'round the house and entered through the back door to avoid those sleeping. I stepped into the kitchen. Linda was finishing cleaning up the breakfast dishes.

"Did you see an empty coffee can?" I asked.

"No," she replied, "just the full one."

"Wayne needs a coffee can."

"How come?"

"I don't know."

Linda looked out the back window. She saw the small chicken coop.

"Did you check in that shed?" she asked. "Maybe there's something in there you can use."

I headed out.

Wayne and I made our way to the chicken coop. Inside the coop was old and dusty and full of cobwebs and quite possibly fifty-year-old chicken shit. It smelled faintly of sulfur or maybe it was just rotten eggs. Some rickety shelves had been hung that held various odds and ends, along with some ancient paint cans. Nestled with the paint cans were some rusting coffee cans with paint inside that had dried about the time God created colors.

Wayne found the one he wanted and grabbed it. "This'll be perfect," he said.

Wayne and I jogged along the road with the coffee can.

"What's the coffee can for?" I asked.

"Earl needs it," Wayne said. "For a launching pad."

We left the road and made our way through the trees to a small meadow and stream. Waiting there was Earl, Wayne's older brother. Earl was about twelve years old at the time, just as handsome as Wayne 'though more blond and with longer locks. The girls all liked Earl and he in turn liked them back.

Wayne showed the can to Earl. "Will this do?" Wayne asked.

Earl nodded. "Fill it with water," Earl told Wayne, "'bout half way."

While Wayne went down to the stream, I watched Earl work. Earl had a one-pound Hills Bros coffee can with him. He'd punched a small hole with a screwdriver in the bottom of the distinctive red can with its strolling Ethiopian taster walking between the "Hills" and the "Bros." He inserted a firecracker in the hole.

Wayne arrived with the water filled coffee can.

"Wait'll you see this," Wayne said. "It is sooo cool."

Earl took the can from Wayne and placed it on the ground. He checked to see if it was level by looking at the water's meniscus versus the side of the can. He made an adjustment. He checked again and was satisfied.

Earl placed the Hills Bros can with firecracker inside the water filled can. He produced a Zippo from his pocket, flipped it open and thumbed the striker. A flame jumped to life. Earl placed the flame on the fuse and the fuse began to spark.

We took a few steps back then--BOOOOMMMM!!

The firecracker exploded launching the small can thirty to forty feet in the air and casting a spray of water down upon us.

"Whoo hoo!" Wayne shouted. "Let's do that again!"

Wayne trotted to where the Hills brothers had landed. He gathered up the can. It was slightly deformed as the bottom had begun to convex out.

"Man, that was cool!" I said.

Earl turned to me. "Get more water," he said.

I took the painted can down to the stream. Some of the paint had chipped off. I filled the can and headed back.

"Let me do it this time," Wayne said.

Earl pulled another firecracker from his pack and flipped it to Wayne. Wayne wedged the firecracker in the hole in the can and placed it in the launching pad. He took the Zippo from Earl and fired it up. He lit the fuse and flicked the Zippo shut.

KA-BOOOOM!!

We went on like that going through half of Earl's firecrackers. He even let me light one.

After a while as I retrieved the small can I saw that the bottom of the can had convexed nearly to the breaking point. I handed the can to Earl. The hole he'd punched had expanded so much that when Earl tried to put in another firecracker it just slipped on through.

Wayne brought more water while Earl stuffed two firecrackers into the hole and twisted the fuses together. Wayne and I looked on. Earl ignited the Zippo and set it to the bound fuses.

Boom! BOOM!!

The explosions blew the can apart and sent the bottom sailing through the air like a flying saucer.

"Holy crap!" Earl hollered. "It ripped it apart!"

Earl trotted to the Unidentified Flying Coffee can bottom.

Wayne elbowed me. "Let's find a cat and shove one up its ass," he said.

I thought Wayne was crazy, and my expression must have said just that.

Wayne jogged to Earl. "Jimmy thinks we should find a cat and shove one up its ass."

Earl smacked Wayne in the head. "Don't lie, you little bitch," Earl said. "Let's shove one up your ass."

"I'm not lying," Wayne retorted.

Earl turned his back to Wayne. "Yeah, sure you're not" Earl said.

Wayne and I walked along the road heading for home. After some time...

"Why'd you lie?" I asked.

"What," Wayne said. It wasn't a question.

"Why'd you lie to Earl about the cat?"

"Cuz," Wayne shrugged. He walked on.

Wayne had a point there. I never forgot it.

* * *

I sat on the front step of Henry's house and watched the shadows grow long. At the end of one wooden plank that formed the second step someone had long ago carved something, possibly a name. All I could make out was "or" with a curve after the "r" that could have been a "c" or an "e" or maybe a "g". It looked like there had been something before the "or" but I had no idea what. I wondered what it had said. They didn't carve it deep enough and now it had worn down to just a question in the mind of a small boy, seven going on eight.

The Crazy Lady came out of her house. Her slippers created little dust clouds as she shuffled toward the mailboxes. Years of shuffling had excavated a dry grassless trail from her door to the stand of mailboxes. The path she created would be there long after she was gone. She had added something to her ensemble; she had a wig on top of her head that she wore like a hat. It was brown. She looked like a Cossack.

I watched her check her mailbox. Then she looked in one of the others. She pulled out an envelope and studied it. She put it back. She turned and looked at me. She just stood there wrapped in her housedress underneath her hair hat and stared. I grew uncomfortable and looked away. When I looked back she was still staring. That's when I realized she wasn't looking at me. She was staring at something only she could see, something long since gone.

I am she. I am doing it now. Staring at this moment in my life like I have so often. Over and over. Not carving a shallow trail that fades to nothing over time, but tracing it over and over and over until it's a deep rut that won't decay.

Thursday September 3

Mary and I climbed into her car. When I was seven going on eight my mom drove a 1962 Chevy Biscayne station wagon with a six cylinder and a three-on-the-tree. Mary put the key in the ignition, stepped on the clutch and started up the old Blue Flame Six.

I buckled myself in the passenger seat. I had dressed in my "good" clothes; a wrinkled button-down short-sleeved shirt and slacks with worn knees and let-down cuffs. I had even styled my hair by wetting the comb in the bathroom sink, dragging it through the front of my hair and slicking it to one side.

"Did I tell you you're looking mighty dapper this morning?" Mary said.

I gave her a big gap-toothed grin, which she took with a smile.

"I flossed," I said.

"So you did."

Mom hooked the gearshift lever with her little finger, pulled it close to her and lifted to ease it into reverse. The lever resisted and quivered before giving in and finding its way into reverse. Mom backed away from the house. She disengaged the clutch and pulled the gearshift down for first. While still rolling slowly backward Mary eased the clutch out, we stopped then moved forward. She cranked the steering wheel hard and aimed us down the road to visit my dad.

We headed out of town. I couldn't see much from the window, mostly just the telephone wire descending and rising from pole to pole. Down, up, pole, down, up, pole. Occasionally I'd see a sign or a streetlight. Mary skillfully shifted through the gears. We took the onramp to the freeway. Mary turned on the radio. Freddie Mercury sang about a crazy little thing called love.

My dad was in prison; had been there since before I could remember. I know now that I had just turned four years old when he went to prison. I had glimpses of memories from that time or maybe before, but none of him, so to me he wasn't real. It seemed as though if something happened before I could remember, it may as well have happened a million years ago. Dinosaurs and John Kennedy walking with Jesus in the jungles of Viet Nam on their way to see my dad...in prison.

The freeway was long and straight. It grew hot. I unbuckled my seatbelt, slid to the edge of the seat, reached under the dashboard and pulled the handle for the floor vent. Warm air blew from the vent, but it was better than nothing: no air-conditioning in the big wagon. No power windows for that matter, or power steering or power brakes. The vehicle was designed for one thing, to get you and a bunch of other people and all of their stuff from one place to another. The only amenities were a cigarette lighter that didn't work and an AM radio rocking out Queen.

"You owe your life to one just like that," I remember my Uncle Henry saying to me. We were riding in Henry's truck to pick up alfalfa for Grandma Verdie's horses. She wasn't my grandma nor Henry's, but that's what Henry called her. We were riding in Henry's truck, me kneeling on the bench seat by the passenger window, and Henry operating the truck, less like driving and more like conducting a symphony of double clutches and shifters and accelerators, and Henry was pointing to a bright red Pontiac convertible. "A candy-apple red '68 Pontiac Bonneville ragtop, yessir I remember that car," Henry said. His eyes danced in delicious memory and I wanted some of that and so I stared at the big red convertible too. I was remembering him talking while I rode next to my mom in her station wagon just as I'm remembering it right now. A memory in three slices of time. And Henry's thirty-year-old truck seemed so much older to me than a thirty-year-old truck seems to me now. Even riding beside my mom in the summer of 1981 in her Chevy, Henry's truck seemed ancient 'though it was but nine years older than Mary's station wagon. Henry's pick-up was Paleolithic. "Your dad drove a Bonneville just like that one the day he met your mom. He was cruising the boulevard and she was waiting at the crosswalk when he came to a stop and she said 'nice car.' That, compadre, is how your parents met." So I owe my life to a candy-apple red convertible, I suspect I'm not the only one.

I rested my head against the armrest on the door and fell in and out of sleep. My hair dried while I was lying this way. It stuck straight up in front like Elmo Tuttle from the "Blondie" comic strip. I would wake up a cartoon character.

Mary downshifted to second and took a corner. She pulled into the prison parking lot and found a place to park. She turned off the ignition.

"Hey," she said. "Wake up. We're here."

We got out of the car and approached the visitor's entrance. My mom talked to a guard. She showed her driver's license and had to have her purse inspected before we could go to the visitor's center. I wasn't sure what my dad did to get himself tossed into prison, but it couldn't have been too bad since mom and I were able visit him without a James Cagney glass partition between us.

The visitor center looked like a small elementary school cafeteria with tables and benches neatly aligned. The walls were painted discount beige. There was a sign that showed the visiting hours, which now seems odd. They didn't have one outside the visitor center and since we were already inside, who was the sign for? There was also a sign that set out reasons visitors could be barred from future visits: 1. Attempting to bring a weapon into a prison. 2. Attempting to bring an unauthorized item other than a weapon into a prison. 3. Charged or convicted of an offense under the following provisions: I couldn't read "the following provisions" because the letters were too small.

Mary sat across from Frank, my dad. I sat next to Frank. Frank was all of twenty-eight then, handsome and optimistic. His hazel eyes flashed when he looked at me. His dark hair brushed the top of his ears and fell over his eyes. Mary reached her hand out to brush the hair from Frank's eyes, but she stopped midway. Her hand gracefully dropped to the table. Frank wore a whisper for a mustache and a patch of hair underlined his bottom lip.

I didn't pay attention to what they were talking about...

"C'mon baby, don't say that," Frank said.

"Don't 'baby' me, Frank," Mom said.

...since I was looking around the room at the various prisoners...

"I can't keep living this way," Mary continued, "Jimmy can't live this way. He doesn't even know you."

"He knows me. He'll get to know me. It's only a little while longer."

"Two years."

...and thinking how it wasn't like in the movies...

"Just two years," Frank said. "Things'll be different, Mare. You'll see."

...I mean I didn't see a single prisoner with a tin cup or harmonica.

"What is it, honey?" Mary said to me.

"I gotta pee," I said.

"I'll take him," Frank offered.

The restroom was a big open space with two stalls without doors, a water trough urinal on one wall and a huge round sink in the middle of the floor. The sink had a steel rail wrapping its base that you stepped on to start the flow of water. Another steel circular rail sprang from the center of the sink that was punched with holes every inch or so. That was where the water came out. The water flowed from every hole even if you were the only one washing your hands: not very economical. The bathroom was painted discount Eggshell. The paint was thick, as though they painted the room at least once a year. A guard stood watch.

Frank and I stood before the urinal. Scattered throughout the trough were a dozen pink urinal cakes in various states of decay. I aimed for one. I looked over at my dad.

"Holy crap!" I'm pretty sure I said out loud.

My dad's dick was huge! How could he walk with that thing? I'm standing there peeing out of a baby carrot and even then I had to move it to cross my legs.

I hadn't yet learned the true meaning of perspective.

"Dad?" I said.

"Yeah."

"Were you a hero?"

"A hero?" Frank asked.

I looked up to his face. "When you were in the army," I said.

Frank looked away.

"I don't talk about that," he said staring at the cheap paint on the wall. He stared a long time. He didn't blink. "I was a Marine," he said.

I looked at Frank for something more; it never came. We put ourselves away and zipped up.

Mary drove the car down the lonely freeway. She stared out the windshield at the road, less a driver than a passenger.

I knelt in the front seat and watched the brown hills of the inner Coast Ranges race by. From time to time billboards would pass advertising food at Sambo's, gas at Union 76 and intrigue at the Winchester Mystery House. It was said ghosts haunted Sarah Winchester. I imagine we all have our ghosts. The story goes that Sarah kept building on to her house for years and years to appease her spirits. I suppose that's one way, if you have the money. Money surely was the least of Sarah's problems. I don't know if the spirits were propitiated; I hope so for her sake.

Sarah Winchester was public about her ghosts; my dad kept his to himself.

On the radio Devo was whipping us. Mary broke her spell and punched one of the radio's buttons. The needle moved down the dial to the oldies station. The song was in mid-play and Bobby Hatfield was singing, "...my darling, I hunger for your touch." When he got to "as time goes by so slowly," Mom turned off the radio. She gripped the steering wheel hard. She was biting on her lip.

When evening came we pulled into a McDonalds for a bite to eat. We sat at a table near the window. Mary absently dabbed a french fry into a glob of ketchup; she'd been at it for a few minutes. I preferred to eat all my fries first because I didn't like them cold. I didn't mind the burger cold. I had eaten my entire bag of fries while Mom dabbed that same fry in the ketchup. Dab...dab, dab... dab. I opened the wrapping of my hamburger. I extracted the pickle from the burger and dropped it on the tray. I licked my fingers.

Four days left and my mom and I had not exchanged one word on the entire trip home. I didn't think about it at the time, but I do now. I could not know what she was going through. I do now and even so, we've never spoken of it.

Mary pulled the car in front of Henry's house. We got out and headed to the door.

I went to my room for bed. I reached under my pillow and took out the tee shirt, my father's tee shirt. I slipped it over my head. I slid under the covers and cut off the fifteen-watt bulb. I laid there in the dark.

That was it--my only memory of my dad. I never saw him again.

Eventually he was released from prison, and soon thereafter was found dead from ethanol poisoning. He drank himself to death. What a stupid way to die. I didn't learn about it until months after he died. I guess that since they were no longer married, people just didn't think to tell mom, or me. A cousin of Mary's sent her a newspaper clipping in a birthday card. Happy Birthday Mary.

I was left with the memory I just told you about. And this one:

Sometime later that night I heard soft murmuring coming from the other room. I carefully got out of bed and silently approached and opened the door.

From the shadows in the hall I saw Mary sitting in the dark on the hide-a-bed. She was weeping. I just watched.

That was the last time I saw her cry. She cried a long time. She cried out a quarter century of tears that night, maybe more.

Friday, September 4

The morning was already heating up. I mounted my bike and headed off to face the day. The Crazy Lady had already been out to the mailboxes and was shuffling back to her house empty-handed as I rode past. She eyed me good. I turned left at the end of the block.

In the distance the drone of a lawnmower engine was carried on the breeze.

It's funny how even now just the sound of a gas lawnmower leads my thoughts to this place. I'll hear it and my mind goes to this day and this time riding my bike on an empty road at the close of summer. And although I'm not sad when I first hear the lawnmower, and I wasn't sad when this memory was born, I'll feel despair in the remembering. Memories bring crushing emotions and create despair--if God has ever cursed man, memories are surely it. I am cursed, you see, because I know how the story ends.

The sound of the lawnmower engine grew while I pedaled down the worn road. The aging blacktop was a vascular system of ancient cracks, some filled long ago with tar that webbed up and down and across the narrow road. I cycled near an empty field surrounded by a barbed wire fence; the small cemetery was visible in the distance. The cemetery was void of activity; slumbering.

In the field was a kid riding a mini-bike; I had found the source of the lawnmower sound. It was Matt, 'though we didn't call him that. I'm pretty sure only the teachers at school called him Matt. Matt was in my grade, but nearly a year older. He was blond and somewhat plump, his pullover shirt never quite pulled over his belly. He was the only kid in class with a mini-bike and we all wanted to ride it. I stopped and straddled my bike and watched him ride. Matt rode with his left hand on the handlebars and his right down at the engine working the accelerator on the carburetor.

Matt spotted me and aimed the mini-bike in my direction. I dismounted and let my bike fall where it was, embraced by weeds. I went to the fence and rested my foot on the bottom strand of barbed wire. Matt pulled up to the fence and cut the engine.

"Hey," I said.

"Hey."

"Can I ride it?"

"No, probably wouldn't be safe, I broke the accelerator cable," he explained. "But you can hop on back."

Matt scooted forward in the seat while I made my way under the barbed wire.

Matt pulled the rope to start the mini-bike. I climbed on back and we were off. We rode like Pony Express riders on the three and a half horsepower mini metal steed, down small gullies and over tiny rounded hills. The wind blew our hair back and blew smiles on our faces. The engine hiccupped then smoothed out. We raced over a washboard section and my teeth rattled in their sockets. Tears seeped from the corners of my eyes and traced wet trails to my ears.

At the far end of the field there was a small wooden gate. Matt steered us through it and out on to the road. The mini-bike coughed a couple of times. We just completed the turn toward the direction of my bike when the mini-bike sputtered out its remaining bit of gas. We coasted for a stretch then came to a stop.

We dismounted and I wiped away the tear tracks. We knew then the meaning of 'gas shortage.' We pushed the mini-bike to where I dropped my bicycle. I picked up my bike and we looked down the long road.

So on that sleepy summer morning we pushed our bikes back home. The lazy sun took forever to rise and it felt like the whole world was on government time and it had clocked out and gone to lunch. It seemed like it would always be summer and I would always be seven going on eight. God, how little I knew.

We arrived at Matt's house. The garage door was open and Matt's brother Mike was working under the hood of a car in the driveway.

On the lawn was Matt's five-year-old nephew Billy. Billy had been Mike and his long-gone girlfriend's surprise package. Billy was seated in a cardboard box with the front and rear flaps folded in. Billy was wearing a motorcycle helmet much too large for him and had the cup to an athletic supporter upside down and pressed against his face.

"Rogue Six to Rogue One," Billy muffled through the cup. "Go ahead Rogue Six," he answered himself. "I've got Vader and have him in my sights, I'm going in for the kill."

"Hey Billy," Matt asked, "where are your wings?"

Billy tapped on the side flaps of the cardboard box.

Matt turned to me. "That's Billy," he said, "my retard nephew."

Matt himself was a surprise. His brother Mike was maybe fifteen years older. Mike raced enduro motorcycles on weekends and was an auto mechanic by trade. He wore his grease-covered hands as badges of honor. Women loved him because he could fix anything, but they secretly cringed when those black stained fingers slid past feminine navels on their way to the warm secret places.

Mike went into the garage. I rested my bike on the lawn while Matt pushed the mini-bike into the garage. I followed.

Mike was searching within a grease covered cigar box full of loose nuts and bolts.

"Hey Mike," Matt said.

"Yo Porknoodle," Mike replied. "Get me the quarter drive ratchet and sockets would ya?"

That's what we called Matt. Porknoodle. I cannot believe how incredibly insensitive we were. I don't know who gave him the name or how I first heard it. He was just always Porknoodle. He wasn't alone. There was a kid in the neighborhood who'd been badly burned in a fire. He was unrecognizable. We called him French Fry. To his face. As if that was his real name. French Fry and Porknoodle...Christ. We are all going to hell.

Matt walked to the workbench, grabbed a socket set and handed it to Mike. Matt and I headed into the house.

We came in through the kitchen. Matt's kitchen was an explosion of Antique Gold and chickens. The stove, the dishwasher, the refrigerator, even the toaster all Antique Gold. The counter held a porcelain chicken cookie jar, chicken salt and pepper shakers (I believe the pepper was actually a rooster) chicken hand towels, chicken potholders and a chicken breadbox. Matt went directly to the Antique Gold refrigerator and opened it.

"You want something to drink?"

"Sure," I said.

Matt took out a container of orange juice and a plastic kit. He set them both on the counter and pulled two glasses from the cupboard. He poured the juice and handed me one of the glasses.

Matt took a small sip of juice then opened the plastic kit. Inside was a hypodermic needle and vial of insulin. Matt checked the needle, pulled his shirt up and stuck himself in the stomach.

Matt was diabetic and that made him the strongest kid I knew. He gave himself a shot in the stomach everyday. Man, I'd freak at just the thought of having to see a doctor and Matt stuck himself everyday. Everyday. That's strength.

We took our juice to the living room. One wall was a testament to Mike's motorcycle prowess, a few dozen trophies and plaques. Nearby a small lone BMX trophy sat on a bookcase.

"Check this out," Matt said.

Matt handed me the BMX trophy.

"I won it this past June," Matt continued. "Pretty cool huh."

"Way cool."

"Thought I'd bring it to school for show and tell."

"That'd be cool. I should find something to bring."

I thought of my dad's medal.

※ ※ ※

On my way home, I slowly rode past Karen's house. Through the window I could see Karen setting the table for dinner. She wore a white barrette over her ear to keep the hair from her eyes. She moved gracefully from place to place, setting silverware around plates.

A few years earlier Karen's dad built her a playhouse in their backyard, complete with electricity, drywall and trim. It was really cool. It had a Dutch door that opened into the main room. There was a small kitchen where Karen served us 60-watt cupcakes from her Easy Bake Oven. It was there in that small kitchen where we had our first kiss, our only kiss. We puckered our lips as tightly as we could and pressed them together. Neither one of us made the smacking noise. Just a soft and silent kiss.

I pedaled towards home.

As I neared my street I saw an early seventies Mercury Comet all jacked-up in the back with huge oversize rear tires approaching. The Mercury slowed. Sharon drove the Merc with Mary in the passenger seat. They were dressed for a night of cheap beer and sweaty bikers. Mary rolled down her window. I rode up to the car.

"We'll be late," Mary said. "Henry's not home yet. You handle dinner?"

I nodded.

"Be good!" Sharon hollered as she gunned the engine and roared off.

I watched them go. I pushed on the pedal and headed for home. I coasted up to the house. Sitting on the steps were Angie and Amy. Amy carried a drawing pad and a crayon colored cigar box filled with crayon remains. Near them were a couple of backpacks.

I dropped the bike and headed to the door.

"Hey Jimmy," Angie said.

"Hey Angie."

"Your mom said you were gonna cook dinner."

"Yep."

I entered the house with Angie right on my heels, as was her wont. Amy quietly followed dragging the backpacks; she left them just inside the door.

I went to the pantry and removed a can of tuna fish, a box of macaroni and cheese and a can of cream of mushroom soup. I set them on the counter and found a saucepan. Angie followed me like her shadow was sewn to my feet.

"What are you making?" Angie asked.

"Macaroni and cheese."

I filled the saucepan with water and set it on the stove. I lit a wooden match, turned on the gas for one of the burners on the stove and set the match to it. The flame jumped from the match and curled around the burner.

I got out the can opener.

"That's not how my mom makes it," Angie said.

"Mine either," I replied.

I opened the box, removed the cheese packet and poured the noodles in the saucepan.

Amy entered quietly, the drawing pad and crayons in tow, and sat at the small table. She took out a few crayons and began to draw.

"My uncle Henry makes it this way," I explained. "It's good."

I stirred the orange powdery "cheese" into the noodles. Angie opened the soup while I forked out the tuna into the macaroni and cheese. I slopped the soup into the tuna, macaroni and cheese mixture. Amy continued to draw. I climbed up on the counter and took plates from the cabinet. Angie placed silverware on the table. Amy finished her drawing--a depiction of my old duct-taped tennis shoes hanging over the wire.

We sat at the table quietly eating. After a while...

"I know a joke," I said.

Angie looked to me. Amy continued eating.

"Why do elephants wear red tennis shoes? Say why," I said.

"Why?" Angie complied.

"To hide in cherry trees. You ever see an elephant in a cherry tree?"

"No."

"See, it works."

Angie smiled.

After our scrumptious and nutritious meal "we" cleaned up. I stood on a chair and washed the dishes while Angie stood on the floor next to me and played with the soap bubbles. Amy sat at the table.

Henry and Linda came home later that evening. They let us stay up late. Henry made popcorn and, while we watched The Tonight Show starring Johnny Carson, he taught us how to catch the white fluffy kernels in our mouths; Henry was quite skilled at it. Henry, Angie and I sat at the edge of Henry's bed and shared a bowl of popcorn. Blue light from the television flickered across our faces. Linda sat upright in the bed and watched TV between us. Amy sat by herself in a beanbag chair next to the bed. She ate from her own small bowl and looked out the window to the night sky.

"Henry," Linda said, "you're getting popcorn all over the bed."

"Life is a bed of popcorn," Henry crunched.

"Roses, it's a bed of roses."

"Not my life," Henry said. "How about yours?"

Linda thought. "So far," she said, "just manure before planting roses."

"Then popcorn is better."

Linda took a kernel from the bed, tossed it and caught it in her mouth.

"Popcorn is better," she laughed.

At bedtime I pulled the hide-a-bed out and made it up. Angie and Amy, in their nightgowns, climbed in. I turned out the light.

I went to my room and put on the big tee shirt. I climbed under the covers, switched off the small light and resolved to stay awake until Mom came home. This was a sure-fire way to insure I'd be asleep in less than two minutes.

Sometime during the night in the still darkness Mary quietly came home and found the twins asleep in her bed. She crawled into bed next to Amy.

Even our dreams were unaware there were only three days left.

James C. Wolf

Saturday, September 5

The morning light peeked into my room. I softly awakened. As I broke the spell of sleep I saw a small hand draped across my shoulder. Angie was asleep next to me in the bed.

I carefully slipped out of bed. I noticed Angie's white cotton underpants were bunched on the floor. My tee shirt was twisted around me like a cocoon. I unwound myself and silently butterflied my way out of the room.

I surveyed the living room. Mary slept in the hide-a-bed, one foot sticking out from under the covers. Amy had moved to the chair and was curled up asleep, a pillow resting over her in place of a blanket.

Angie came up beside me. Her small hand slipped into mine and I let it stay there. I don't know why.

A short time later Angie, Amy and I sat at the small kitchen table and quietly downed some Lady Lee cereal. Plink. Our spoons plinked against the bowls. Plink. Amy barely ate while she drew with her crayons. Plink. The rest of the house still slept. Plink. I could hear Alex snoring through the wall upstairs. Plink. Milk dripped a little from my mouth and I wiped it with my sleeve.

Angie stopped plinking. She stared into her cereal bowl. "Can we stay here?" she asked.

I stopped plinking and looked at her. Her eyes met mine. They were insistent, pleading. Amy stopped drawing.

"Can we stay here...live here?" Angie asked again. "We don't like it at home. Mom's boyfriends, they.... Can you ask your mom?"

Amy held the crayon just off the paper.

I didn't know what to say.

Angie followed Mary and Sharon out the front door. Amy stood at the door, backpack strapped across her shoulders, crayons and drawing pad in one hand, in her other she held one of her drawings.

I watched from the kitchen doorway.

"Amy!" Sharon yelled. "Come on!"

Amy's eyes met mine for the first time. She dropped the drawing and headed out.

I crossed the room and watched them leave. I picked up the drawing and looked at it. It was a drawing of a cherry tree, an elephant's gray trunk hung like a seven year-old below a branch.

❊ ❊ ❊

I walked along the side of the road wearing the boonie and an old backpack. I stopped and dug up a cola bottle that was half buried in the dirt. I always felt like maybe I should wash the dirt from the bottles before redeeming them for cash. I'd seen people taking bottles in to the store that looked brand new, so clean and free of dirt, like a glassblower had just created them. My bottles were always covered with dirt or dust or even cobwebs. No one ever said they were supposed to be clean and they gave me money all the same, but I somehow felt that the clerk thought my bottles were inferior.

I opened the backpack and placed the bottle inside. It clinked against the three other bottles I had already collected. I saw another bottle across the road. I crossed over only to find that it was only an empty wine bottle.

I should have asked my mom if Angie and Amy could stay with us. I should have asked and they would have stayed and maybe their demons would have abated. And maybe because they would be there, I would have been too distracted to go to the attic. Too distracted to kneel. And I would be someone different altogether. But I didn't ask Mary.

Once you know something you can never un-know it. You've always known and always will. I didn't understand the importance of what Angie had asked. I understand now. I've always understood.

I spied Wayne walking up the old two-lane highway. Wayne carried a couple of empty Clorox bottles.

I watched him walk; I did not call out to him. I didn't know why at the time. Our friendship had reached its apex and had begun its slow decline. It wouldn't have mattered much because I would never see him again after. Before and after. Then he spotted me.

Wayne lifted one of the Clorox bottles as a wave. "Hey Jimmy!" he called.

Wayne huffed it up to the corner to where I stood. He sported a fresh and crescent shaped bruise that hugged the outer edge of his left eye and extended down his cheekbone. It was red and blue; it hadn't yet started to yellow.

"What happened to your eye?" I asked.

"Bill hit me."

I waited for him to go on. He didn't. Sometimes he was that way--answer only the question, wait for the next question, answer, then the next question, answer, and so on. I don't know why he did that.

"Where you going?"

"Out to the dam."

"Why?"

"Gonna slide down the spillway. Come with me, you can use this bottle."

I wasn't sure I wanted to go anywhere with Wayne.

"I don't know," I said. "It's pretty far."

"We'll hitch."

I adjusted my backpack and we set out.

As we walked we heard a car coming. We turned and while walking backward stuck out our thumbs. The car zoomed passed. We turned back.

"Why'd your step-dad hit you?" I finally asked.

"Just cuz I took some money."

We walked on. I'm pretty sure "took some money" meant "stole some money." Wayne saw it differently.

"It wasn't like he was using it," Wayne added. "It was just a bunch of real old quarters and half dollars that he kept in his drawer."

Wayne looked up into the sun and shaded his eyes.

"I figure they'll buy me a new bike," he said.

"What?"

"Maybe a ten speed."

"You get in trouble and they get you a bike?"

A car approached. We turned, thumbs extended. The car drove passed. We turned back.

"Not a bad deal actually," Wayne said.

"Why would they get you a bike?"

"My mom will feel sorry for me and 'll get mad at Bill," Wayne explained. "And he'll feel all guilty for hitting me and have to make it up to me. It's worked before."

The sun rose high as we walked along. Minutes turned into hours as the heat bore down on the two of us while we trudged to the dam. We had both shed our shirts; mine hanging partway out of my backpack, Wayne's draped over his head.

A car approached only now we didn't turn around. We merely stuck out our thumbs. The car didn't stop. We never did catch a ride. I guess we too closely resembled the infamous pre-teen Clorox bottle serial killers of Duncan's Landing.

❊ ❊ ❊

The small dam and reservoir was one of a series built in the mid-thirties. Through the main entrance there is a gravel parking lot, a ranger's station and campgrounds. The campgrounds include a play area for kids. I'd been to it a few times. There were trails from the campgrounds that went around the reservoir that were lined with sycamore, cottonwood and big-leaf maple trees. In the winter there would be tiny waterfalls on the trail. Spring brought wildflowers to the meadows and woods. There is a short section of fence blocking off the spillway. To get to the spillway we had to cut through Luccesi Ranch to the west and climb through coyote

169

brush, poison oak and sagebrush. The spillway drops twenty to twenty-five feet but felt like a mile to a seven year old, even one going on eight. The spillway always seemed to be crying, its tears running down its face and forming a small deep pond at its base.

Wayne put his shirt back on, took a Clorox bottle and while grasping the handle sat on it and crushed it flat. I watched him while I slipped my shirt on. I replicated Wayne's actions and flattened my Clorox bottle.

Wayne worked his way out to the small flow of water emanating from the spillway. He carefully sat on the bottle grasping the handle between his legs. He leaned back, lifted his legs, slid down the spillway and skipped across the small pond at the bottom. He sank under the water and came splashing up all excitement and smiles.

Then it was my turn. Following Wayne's lead, I slid down the spillway and skipped across the water. I went under and came up gasping for air. Wayne splashed me. We swam to shore and scampered back up the face of the spillway.

Wayne went down with both hands raised in the air.

I started down but inadvertently spun around and ended up going down backward.

I slid down but just at the bottom I planted my shoe covered feet and dove into the water.

Wayne slid down on his knees, a Clorox bottle under each one.

The sun had crested and begun its descent. Wayne and I spread out on the face of the spillway and let the warm sun dry us off.

"I'm getting thirsty," I said.

"Me too," Wayne agreed. "Let's go over to the campgrounds."

We made our way out of Luccesi Ranch to the road and headed to the entrance to the campgrounds. We trudged through the gravel parking lot. There were concrete parking blocks angled in a row indicating where to park. An old pick-up rested in the lot. It hadn't been there long; I could hear the engine ticking as it cooled down. The ranger's station stood at the end of the gravel lot. A small wooden fence separated the lot from the manicured campgrounds. Near the play area we found a drinking fountain.

Wayne drank from the fountain for a long time...too long. I set my backpack on the ground and wiped sweat from my brow. Finally it was my turn. Wayne rested with hands on knees while I drank.

I finished and wiped my mouth with my sleeve. Wayne drank some more water.

I looked up to the sun, the 'boonie' shielding my eyes. "Think we should head back?" I asked.

We trudged along under the blistering sun. I held onto the backpack straps with both hands. Wayne was sluggish; he lagged behind.

"I'm not feeling too good," he said.

"Maybe we'll be able to catch a ride."

I looked around. There wasn't a car in sight.

I stayed off the road, the macadam too hot for my feet. I alternated between walking on the soft shoulder and hiking in the tall grass. When I looked behind me I could see trails where I tromped through grass as proof that I'd been there. I liked it. Proof that we've been somewhere pulls strong. Ask anyone who has ever etched their initials in wet concrete or carved them into trees. Ask anyone who has ever spray painted their name on a wall, or peed their name in the snow. Ask Kilroy.

Wayne slowed considerably. He was growing quite pale.

"I think I need to stop before I barf," he said.

We stopped. Wayne flopped down beside the road in full crucifix position. I sat cross-legged. I quietly looked around. Wayne put his arm across his eyes to block the sun. I saw the big orange ball of a Union 76 gas station maybe a half a mile away.

"There's that gas station at the corner," I said. "I could go get some help."

Wayne didn't answer.

I stood and adjusted my backpack. I took the boonie from my head and dropped it on Wayne's stomach. Wayne placed it over his face. I headed out.

I arrived at the old service station. It only had two pumps, one hand labeled "Ethyl" and the other "Reglar". I could see that under "Reglar's" hand lettering, the sign had read "Royal." There were some rusting cars in various states of disrepair littering the lot.

In the service bay, I found the gas station attendant under the hood of a Buick. The Buick had an old and fading "76" antenna ball. The ball was so old it didn't have the white outline around the "7" and the "6" that separated them from the orange of the rest of the globe like the new ones.

"Mister?" I asked. "Do you have a phone I can use?"

"There's a pay phone 'round the corner," he said to the carburetor.

I looked around the corner at the old pay phone. I dug into my pockets--empty.

I went back to the service bay.

"Mister? Do you take empties?" I asked.

The attendant wheezed out an exasperated breath. "Man if it ain't one thing..." he said. He yanked a filthy red shop towel from his back pocket and wiped grease onto his hands--at least that's how it looked. He headed to the office. I trailed him.

Inside the office was a wire display rack holding quart cans of Union 76 motor oil. A metal pour spout hung next to the display for use by customers. Drops of oil had dripped on the floor from its pointed opener.

The attendant stepped behind the counter and pressed a button on the cash register. It chinged open.

I lined up the dirt-covered cola bottles on the counter then the attendant dropped a few coins in my palm.

At the pay phone, I slotted a quarter and dialed. The receiver rang a few times. Alex answered the phone.

"Speak to me," Alex said.

"Hey Alex, is my mom or Henry there?"

"Nope, just me. What's the haps?"

"Me and Wayne are coming home from the dam, but now Wayne is sick."

"You and Wayne hiked all the way to the dam in this heat?"

"We tried to hitch but no one stopped," I explained.

"What's wrong with him?" he asked.

"He thinks he's gonna barf and he's all white."

"You guys eat anything?"

"We drank some water. I ate this morning."

"Okay. I think I know what's wrong. Where are you?"

I gave Alex our location in proximity to the gas station. He gave me an estimated time of arrival and rang off. I headed back to Wayne.

In thinking about it now, it feels like karma. I know I didn't think about it then, and I'm sure Wayne never thought about it, but now it feels like what went around was coming around. I believe this was the only time I was around when it did.

I arrived back to where Wayne still lay.

"Alex is coming," I said.

No response.

We heard Alex well before seeing him. The muffler on Alex's car was so bad he might as well not even have had one--perhaps he didn't. I could hear the engine, "rrrrrrrrrrrrrnnnnnnnnnnnnnnnnn" as he drove down the highway and when he let off the gas at the Union 76 station to make the corner his car "blaued." "Blau, blau, blau, blau." "Rrrrrrrrnnnnnnnnnnn, blau, blau, blau!" Alex pulled up in his big sixties Ford Galaxie sedan. Wayne crawled into the back. Alex handed him a bag of Lay's potato chips and a gallon jug of water.

"Eat some of these," Alex said.

Wayne complied.

I got in the front seat. Both front seats were torn and ragged and the stuffing and springs were coming out. Alex had placed two seat cushions, the kind with the wire spring covered by a nylon mesh, over the damaged seats. Alex took the drivers seat, started the car and pulled on to the road. "Rrrrrrrrnnnnnnnnnnnn, blau, blau, blau!"

"Chips will make him feel better?" I asked.

"Salt," Alex replied. "He probably sweated out too much salt."

Wayne ate chips while he lay on the back seat. Chip crumbs dotted his neck and hair and the seat. I reached over the console between the seats and grabbed the jug of water. I took a long drink. I passed the jug to Alex and he took a hit. After a while Wayne sat up and asked for the water.

The drive home felt remarkably short compared to our trip out. Presently Alex pulled up out front of Uncle Henry's house. Alex got out and opened the back door.

"How you feeling?" Alex asked Wayne.

"Better," Wayne answered.

"Good," Alex said. "Then give me some of them chips."

Alex smiled and gummed down on a handful of chips.

The sun set with but two days to go.

Sunday, September 6

Church bells rang calling the faithful to the 10:00 am services. The chimes counted down from ten like God's own rocket launch.

The church sat back from the road in the shade of some great oaks. The whitewashed house of worship had two wings sprouting from either side, so that from above, through God's eyes, it looked like a cross. Out in front of the church a sign read: God has a plan for you.

I straddled my bike across the street from the small community church. I wore the boonie and canteen. It was already a warm day and I wiped sweat from my brow. I drank from the canteen.

Families dressed in their finest clothes filed into the church through large wooden doors, while paying their morning respects to the pastor. Many of the women and girls fluttered away with white folding fans.

As the last of the flock were corralled, I saw two young teenage boys slip out a side door and sneak away from the church. I watched them leave then mounted my bike and followed.

Like Magnum, P.I., I stayed well behind while I trailed them. They walked briskly and didn't look back. The boys were similarly dressed in their Sunday best and I suspected they were brothers. They talked but I couldn't hear what they were saying. One was quite animated; he gestured back toward the church. The other one looked at his watch and said something. Whatever he said calmed gesture boy down.

They turned the corner and their gait slowed to a casual Sunday morning stroll. I reached the corner. I crossed to the east side of the street where I could follow in shadow. I could see them talking, their mouths forming silent words that I wasn't privileged to hear. From time to time a laugh would sneak away from them and float to me and chuckle softly.

I followed them to a small business district. They walked up to Winchell's (Home of the Warm 'n Fresh Donut™) and entered. There the menu board was their sermon and a "raised glazed" their Eucharist.

I ended surveillance and pointed my bike towards home.

There was something beautiful about the boys sneaking away from church together on the last Sunday before school was to start. It was like a last break for freedom, the freedom of summers and youth. The freedom to discover, the freedom to wonder. The freedom to be together as brothers while there was still time. The beautiful freedom of sharing a doughnut and a laugh. For them it would end for the year and, God willing, begin anew the following June. For me, the world would lose all wonder and beauty on what was then the day after tomorrow. No wonder, just the impact of choice. No beauty, just dirt.

I dropped my bike in the yard and headed to Uncle Henry's front door. As soon as the bike hit the dirt I had to pee like a bronze water fountain. I don't know what it was, but it was like my bladder could sense toilet proximity. Twenty yards up the road riding my bike, I didn't have to go whatsoever, ten feet from the door and my bladder's going to explode.

I burst through the door. Mom had gotten up and had made the hide-a-bed. I headed up the stairs. Henry, Linda and Alex were in Henry's room watching television. Alex didn't sound happy. "Ah c'mon!" he complained. I pushed the bathroom door open.

If we had a hygrometer it would have been off the scale. The humidity was so high water was dripping from the walls. Mary rested in the tub, hot steaming water up to her chin, a wet washcloth covered her eyes. She had placed a scented candle on the edge of the tub.

"Who is it?" she said.

"It's me."

She removed the cloth from her eyes. "Hey sweetie," she said. "What are you up to?"

"I need to pee," I danced.

My knees knocked together as I lifted the lid and the seat. I had barely gotten my fly open when "the flood of water came upon the earth." One minute before, I didn't think I had to go; now I didn't think I'd stop.

"That's a lot of pee," mom said.

"I shouldn't 'a had that fifth beer," I replied.

"Funny," she smiled. "What are you doing today?"

"Nothing. What are you doing?"

"Nothing."

I squeezed out the last drop and put myself away. I ran water in the sink. I washed my hands while the water got cold, then I filled the canteen.

"Did you get that from your dad's things?" Mary asked.

"Uh huh," I confirmed.

"I want you to leave his things alone," if only she had said, but she didn't. How could she know?

I dried my hands. She replaced the cloth over her eyes. I stepped out of the bathroom and closed the door. I went into Henry's room.

"What are you watching?" I asked.

Henry and Alex just stared at the television. "Football," Linda offered. "You wanna watch?"

"Sure," I said climbing on the bed next to Henry.

I watched players in white shirts with red numbers and gold pants and helmets slam into players in blue shirts and silver pants and helmets. "Who's playing?" I asked.

"San Francisco and Detroit," Alex said never taking his eyes from the TV screen.

"Who's who?" I asked.

"San Fran is in white," Alex said.

We watched the game. From time to time I would ask questions and Alex or Henry would answer. I found out we were rooting for the San Francisco 49ers to beat the Detroit Lions and I learned about plays and penalties and touchdowns. Alex kept saying "same old niners" but I wasn't sure what he meant. San Francisco lost that day to Detroit. Billy Sims, number 20 for the Detroit team scored two touchdowns.

After the game I wandered out back to the old chicken coop. I found an old Estwing leather handled claw hammer. It was heavy and rugged. The leather had dried at the edges but was still soft in the middle where someone's palm sweat had oiled it over the decades. I looked for a nail to whack. Just my luck, the chicken coop was full of them; nails that had loosened over the years and worked their way out trying to escape. BAM! Back in you go. BAM! There's another one. BAM! I don't believe that there is anything in life that has more clarity than a hammer. A nail protrudes--BAM!--it doesn't. Clear. Simple. The leather felt good in my hand. The simplicity felt good in my arm. The clarity felt good in my heart.

I went in the house through the kitchen. Linda was cooking.

"What were you hammering?" she asked.

"Nails."

I watched Linda busily set the table with places for five. She straightened a setting then stirred something on the stove. I looked at the well-set table.

"Is it someone's birthday?" I asked.

"It's Sunday. I thought we could all sit and eat like a regular family."

"Need help?"

"No, I got it under control."

"Smells good," I said.

Linda smiled.

"Do you like to cook?" I asked.

"I like to eat," Linda said. She took a fork and poked it in a pot on the stove. "I guess it's more than that, I like everyone sitting around the table eating. I like the conversation, being together. You don't get that eating McD's."

I sat at the table. She opened the oven door and peered inside. Looked like a roast to me...or maybe cake.

"When I cook by myself," she continued, "I find it helps relieve stress."

"You want me to leave?" I offered.

"No. I like having you here. What I mean is, when I'm cooking with my mom I can't get anything right. 'That's too much salt,' 'The flame's too high,' 'Not so much garlic.' Whatever I do is just not good enough."

"Is your mom a good cook?"

Linda laughed. "No. Not really," she said.

"Are you?" I asked.

"I like to think so."

"Okay then."

She thought for a bit, leaned down and kissed me on the cheek. I didn't know why.

Alex entered. He saw the table set for five.

"What's the occasion?" he asked.

"Linda says we're eating like a regular family," I replied.

"Ahh," he said.

Mary, Henry, Alex, Linda and I sat around the table silently eating. Linda looked at us one at a time. It was absolutely quiet but for forks tinking against plates. Linda was puzzled. She looked at me; I stifled a smile.

"How come everyone's so quiet?" Linda asked.

Mary hid her smile under her napkin.

"Henry?" Linda said.

Henry quietly chewed. I believe he was counting. He opened his eyes big and stuck up his pointer finger in the "just a moment I need to swallow" gesture.

Linda looked at me.

"Jimmy?" She said.

"What?"

"Why are you so quiet?"

"Alex says this is how regular families eat."

Alex grinned. Linda threw a bread roll at him.

"Cut that out," Linda said.

We all laughed.

The plates were half empty. We were half full. The conversation had flowed and I found myself liking this "regular family" business.

"I went to church today," I said.

"Really," Mary said.

"Not inside," I continued. "I just watched people all dressed up going in. There were bells."

"Calling the flock to salvation," Henry said. "I think Pavlov did an experiment about that."

"Henry. Some people really believe," Linda said.

"I didn't say I didn't believe in God," Henry went on. "Just not too sure about the whole religion slash church thing. Especially after Jim Jones."

Alex poured himself some brandy.

"More Kool-Aid anyone?" Alex asked.

Mary held out her glass.

"I'll take a little, 'brother' Alex," Mary replied.

"They have a sign out front," I said.

"There are signs everywhere," Henry twitched.

"And I saw two guys sneaking out the side door," I continued.

"There you go," Alex said.

"They made a break for it" Henry said. "Good for them."

"It made me think of that movie we saw about the army guys digging a tunnel and that one guy took off on a motorcycle," I said.

"The Great Escape," Alex said. "Great movie. Can't believe McQueen's dead."

"Didn't his character die at the end of that movie?" Mary asked.

"Got thrown in 'the hole'," Alex said.

"Same ending as the bible," Henry noted.

There was one day to go before...and we sat and ate like a "regular" family for the first and last time. Mary told a story about how she broke a glass coffee pot on the counter at work and the hot coffee splashed all over a customer's lap--he did a back flip off the stool, but was all right in the end. We learned that Linda was graduated from Cal Berkeley. Alex said he hadn't had a boyfriend in four years and with the CDC report in July about a couple of dozen gay men coming down with Kaposi Sarcoma, he wasn't sure he'd ever have another boyfriend. Henry questioned what the hell was going on with Anwar Sadat in Egypt. "A few days ago he arrests fifteen hundred artists, journalists and politicians and then yesterday the leader of the Coptic Christians," Henry said. Linda said the whole Middle East was shaky and we should go back to steam or electric powered cars and give up on oil. Mom said it would never work, "American's love their cars more than they love their guns" she said. Henry thought Sadat was in for trouble. We couldn't have known that Sadat would be assassinated in exactly one month.

I don't know if Alex's definition of "eating like a regular family" is right or if it's Linda's. They are both foreign to my experience either before or after. What I am sure of: it was the best meal I ever ate.

Monday, September 7

I stared expectantly at the toaster. I could see my reflection in its chrome side. The sides of the toaster were slightly convex and the image staring back at me was wide and distorted. Actually I preferred the concave reflection found in a spoon, because that turned me upside-down.

In the living room Mary was still asleep in the hide-a-bed. I had spotted several other unidentified folks sleeping wherever available but I hadn't bothered to count how many.

The toast popped up. It was one slice, an end piece. We would bypass the first slice of bread and pick out just middle pieces until all that remained were the two ends. I buttered up the toast then sprinkled a little cinnamon and some sugar on it. I took a bite.

When I popped the last bite of toast into my mouth I wiped my hands on my cutoffs. I went to the living room and gingerly stepped around and over sleeping bodies as I made my way to Mary.

"Mom?" I whispered. "School starts tomorrow."

Mary stirred, barely awake.

"Take some money from the mug," she said to the pillow.

I went back to the kitchen and opened a drawer. In the back of the drawer was a coffee mug from the truck stop filled with coins--mom's tips. You don't see people leaving coins for tips much anymore. They mostly leave bills or add a few bucks to their credit card slip. I liked the coins. They were solid and sang in your pocket as you walked. They were like treasure. Treasure is always coins--gold coins in an old trunk buried under an "X" in the sand. I dug a handful of treasure from the mug and shoved it into my pocket.

I mounted the mutt-bike and headed east into the sun. My destination was Kmart way out by the freeway. In many towns residents have to call the freeways by their number--the 495, the I-5, the 215--but in Duncan's Landing it was and still is called just "the freeway." The freeway was about twelve miles from Henry's and would take me a little over an hour to get there if I rode at a decent clip.

I cut through the field to save time. The ruts and rocks in the worn trail shook through to my marrow but sometimes your marrow needs a shaking. The field spilled me out near the Sunshine Super and I turned towards Main Street.

Main Street was once the epicenter for the tremor of business in Duncan's Landing until the freeway was finished sometime in the seventies. Business then sprouted along the freeway like trees to a stream and fed off the flow of automobiles. Main Street lost some merchants to the exodus, but the post office, police station, library and city hall remained. The forsaken merchant buildings became home to real estate offices, barber shops and craft stores. Smatterings of cars were parked diagonally along Main Street as I rode past.

The parking lot at Kmart was filled with other last minute back-to-school shoppers. Cars prowled like hungry lions looking for parking spots near the doors. I rode by heading for the bike-rack.

Henry said the Kmart used to be in town and was called Kresge's. He worked there as a stock boy and wore a patch on his smock that had a red stacked double "S" next to a blue "K" for S.S. Kresge. Henry didn't much care for Kmart, he liked Kresge's better. He liked stores that had real names, names of their founders, because it felt to him like they were run by people, not by corporations. I guess he thought about it a lot. I didn't give it too much thought; I just needed some supplies.

I placed my bike in the rack and headed inside. Kmart was packed with parents and kids doing their last minute back-to-school shopping. I wandered through the store. Parents and clerks helped uncooperative kids as they tried on clothes and shoes.

I watched shopping carts file by that customers had stuffed with new supplies and new clothing and new backpacks and new lunch boxes and such. They rattled past like the Burlington Northern on their way to the vast sea of cashiers. Customers filled their carts and emptied their wallets. I found a well-picked-over display of school supplies.

At the check out line, I bought a five-pack of Ticonderoga pencils-

-number 2, and a Pedigree eraser.

* * *

I piloted my bike 'round the corner to my street. I held the small bag from Kmart in my left hand and steered with my right. I was passed by an old small school bus, painted white. I rode up to Henry's house and dropped my bike in the front yard. I went to the outside faucet. I turned it on and drank straight from the hose.

The Crazy Lady was out in front of her house struggling with a box of groceries. Printed on the side of the box read "Stony Point Methodist Church." She looked around and spotted me.

"You there," she called out.

"Me?" I said.

"Help me carry these groceries."

I shut the water off and set the Kmart bag on the front porch.

I walked over and looked at the groceries, then at the Crazy Lady, then back to the groceries. Helping her carry the groceries meant me carrying the groceries and tailing her into the house. I hefted the box and followed her.

The Crazy Lady's yard was a hodgepodge of unfinished ideas. A shaky old arbor, planters with dying plants and thriving weeds, a fountain that didn't work that held a brackish brown water (Hoboke and Crocus) ripe for raising mosquitoes and a small seemingly misplaced garden with beautiful red tomatoes.

"My husband used to carry the groceries, but he died," she said.

"Must have been a lot of groceries," I observed.

We got to the front step and she opened the door. In the entryway were coats on hooks, an umbrella, woman's slippers just like the ones the Crazy Lady had on, and an old pair of men's work boots. They looked like the oldest boots in the world. Boots that had died, mummified and turned to dust right there on that very spot.

"When did he die?" I asked.

"Long time now..." she said as she shuffled down the hall and disappeared around the corner.

I put the box on the floor next to God's boots.

The Crazy Lady reemerged with an Old Masters cigar box. I watched closely as she opened it; it held coins. She dug out some change and closed the box.

"...long time," she mumbled. "So long now I'm not sure if I ever knew what it felt like."

"Knew what 'what' felt like?"

"To be loved."

I looked at her. "I love you," I should have said. But I didn't.

She slipped me a couple of quarters and followed me out.

We walked past the garden and out to the street. As I went on my way she opened her mailbox and looked inside: waiting for a valentine from heaven.

❊ ❊ ❊

That night after I had gotten ready for bed I placed the pencils and eraser into my backpack. I went into one of the boxes and took out my good clothes. I shook them loose and spread them out in an effort to remove the wrinkles.

I climbed into bed. I turned off the light switch and summer ended. I don't believe it's ever returned.

Tuesday, September 8

The low morning sun shone softly through the attic window casting beams of light through the length of the room that drowsily stretched and landed on my sneakers. I had quietly crept through Uncle Henry's room while he and Linda slept and hoisted myself into the attic. Wearing my good clothes, I tiptoed my way across the attic to my dad's footlocker. It was the first day of school and I was going to bring something for show and tell.

My two-sizes-too-large sneakers were cotton and the floor delicate embracing clouds, muffling all sound. I was a dormouse, silently moving Henry's 15-puzzle boxes. I was a still mountain lake sending nary a wave from the attic to Henry and Linda's sleeping ears. Soon I had exposed the World War Two vintage footlocker.

I knelt before the footlocker like an altar and slowly, ceremoniously raised the lid. Partway up it cried a painful creak and I held my breath. I was a marble statue holding open the lid listening fiercely. Nothing. The marble softened and I hoisted the lid the rest of the way. I took out the small jewelry case and opened it. The Purple Heart was just as I left it. It sparkled with promise. I didn't know then, and don't know now what happened that resulted in awarding my dad the Purple Heart. What I did know then was that they don't give out medals for nothing. I knew that my dad did something to earn the medal while he was in the war. So even if I had nothing to "tell" I knew I had something to "show."

I began to close the lid but stopped when I caught a glimpse of the cigar box. "The quarters" I remembered. I reached into my pocket and pulled out the quarters I got from the Crazy Lady. She got them out of a cigar box. I wondered.

I went back in to the footlocker and moved my dad's gear around until I was able to lift out the cigar box. It was heavy. I nurtured it open. Inside the box, swathed in blue cloth, was a 32-caliber revolver.

I know now that the last thing you'll find in a cigar box is cigars.

I lifted the gun and looked it over. It smelled like 3in1 oil. I could see my face in all its amazement reflected in the pistol's gleaming surfaces.

I had planned to bring the Purple Heart for show and tell. I had planned to talk about my dad the war hero.

I pointed the gun out the window and quietly made a sound like a pistol shot. "P-cue, P-cue." I moved the gun to eye level to sight it. I drew the gun down on Henry's truck, then over to mom's station wagon, then up to the mailbox stand. I didn't pull the trigger.

At that moment I still could have chosen to bring the medal. I could have put the gun back in the cigar box and learned a lesson about cigar boxes and what may or may not be in them. I could have put the cigar box back in the footlocker where it would safely wait for my dad once he was released from prison. I could have shown the medal at school and kids would "oo" and "aw" while I stood before them during my turn at what would have been mostly show and very little tell. Such is the irresistible appeal and power of hindsight, and why we can become so mired in it. Am I the sum of my choices? Are we all?

I replaced the gun in the cigar box. I closed the lid to the footlocker, the Purple Heart inside. A choice forever made in steel.

Who would I be today if I had taken the medal? What would I think? What would I feel?

Cigar box in hand, I crawled out of the attic.

I spread peanut butter then jelly over one half of the last end piece of bread. I folded it over and stuffed it into a sandwich bag. I put the cigar box in my backpack, then the sandwich. I slung the backpack over my shoulder, crept past Mary sleeping unaware on the hide-a-bed and set out for school.

It was still officially summer and would be so for nearly two more weeks, but I felt the eyes of autumn watching as I walked past the mailboxes. The Crazy Lady was already out faithfully checking the mail. She opened one mailbox; looked inside, closed it then opened another.

I turned the corner. An orange tabby watched me with pale-green emotionless eyes from up in a tree. It slowly closed then reopened its eyes the way cats do, seeming to say, "I know more than you" or "I couldn't care less." Two scrubbed teenagers, a boy and girl, got into a bright red Chevy Nova. The car started and drove off. I could hear the trills and buzzes of a wren's call coming from a scrubby thatch of low shrubs. I left the street and cut through a field on a long-worn path.

Butterflies drunkenly flittered from blossom to blossom of sweet-scented crème colored Beargrass flowers. It was as though the whole world was fresh and innocent. Maybe I was seeing things more clearly. Or maybe I just remember with the last brilliant colors of my mind's palate.

The field butted up to a six-foot chain link fence that surrounded the school. I worked my tennis shoes through the links and scaled the fence. I slung my right leg over the top, crossed my left leg over and dropped into the schoolyard.

I walked down the open hallway of the school. Kids, all dressed in new school clothes, played on the playground or huddled in small groups renewing friendships and talking about their summer. It was the first day of third grade. I headed for Miss Johnson's classroom.

I rounded the corner and saw a dozen or so children gathered around the door. Some kids lived nearby; others came on an early bus. We weren't allowed to go into the classroom until the teacher arrived. We would leave our backpacks or lunch boxes or books lined up along the wall near the door while we played or talked or just did nothing.

I approached the classroom. Gathered there were Bill, Steve, Matt whom we called Porknoodle, Jennifer, Heather, Nicole, the other Matt whom we called Matt, Jessica, Karen, Amy, Angie and Wayne. I remember it like it was right now. I could tell you what each was wearing, the color of their eyes, the order their bags were lined up. Amy stood a little away from the other kids. The boys along with Angie were grouped in a loose circle. I joined them.

Matt was showing the BMX trophy he won. The other Matt took it from him to look at.

"Man, it's heavy," the other Matt said.

"See, it's got my name on it," Matt replied.

"That's cool," said the other Matt.

"Can I hold it?" Angie asked.

The other Matt looked to Matt. Matt gave a small shrug. The other Matt handed the trophy to Angie.

"I brought something," I said.

I knelt down and set my backpack on the walk and unzipped it. I pulled out the cigar box and opened it. I took the gun out with two hands and stood to show the others. They looked on in awe.

"Whoa," Wayne said. "Let me see it."

"It's my dad's," I said.

I held the gun out, not pointing, my thumb on the grip, my pointer finger on the trigger, my middle finger on the trigger guard.

Wayne reached for the gun, his fingers touched mine and he said, "Is it lo—"

POW!! The gun went off.

The report echoed through the hall. It was the only sound. The echoes faded to nothing, replaced by ringing in my ears.

It was like watching in slow motion. The bullet exited the muzzle at twelve hundred feet per second. The force of the recoil sent the gun sprawling out of my hand. A startled Angie jerked and dropped the trophy. The trophy broke when it hit the cement. We were all stunned.

In that heartbeat my childhood ended.

The gun landed, skidded along the walk and came to a stop near the grass. One of the girls shrieked. The shriek itself grabbed me by my ears and turned my head.

I looked to Amy. She was covered in blood. Amy looked down. I followed her look.

On the ground a few feet from Amy lay Karen, shot through the neck and bleeding badly.

I looked to Wayne who was frozen in shock. My eyes moved to Matt. Matt met my gaze. He understood. Matt took off running.

"Help!" he cried. "We need help!"

I rushed to Karen, dropped to my knees and pressed my hands against her throat to stem the flow. Blood seeped through my fingers. Karen's eyes locked on mine. Blood pooled around us and soaked into my pants and shoes.

"I'm sorry!" I yelled. "I'm sorry!"

Blood continued to flow between my fingers. Older kids began to arrive.

"I'm sorry! I'm sorry!"

Mr. Svinth was the first teacher to arrive. He pronounced his name Swenth. I remember his short-sleeved sky blue button down shirt adorned with a navy and yellow diagonally striped tie. He was one of the few teachers who still wore a tie. He grabbed me by my shirt and pulled me away from Karen, ripping my shirt vertically on the right side about two inches from the buttons. I landed on my butt on the hard smooth concrete surface of the hall. Mr. Svinth took my place applying pressure to Karen's gaping wound. It was then that I saw her eyes close.

I didn't move sitting there just a few feet from Karen while other teachers began to arrive along with the head custodian, Mr. Tegley.

It was Mr. Tegley who retrieved the gun, my father's pistol. I saw him take a pair of pliers from his tool belt and used them to pick up the gun by the trigger guard.

Angie had left the boys and had gone to her twin. Amy, arms raised in surrender, turned away from her. The shriek I'd heard had been Amy's, the only sound I ever heard her make. Witness to horror, covered in blood, still Amy silently rejected everything, even comfort from her sister.

By then it seemed as though every student and teacher in the school had arrived. Somewhere in the confusion and chaos Wayne had disappeared. I heard teachers asking if the police had been called. Yes. Is there an ambulance on its way? I don't know I think the police will notify them. Do we know who did it? Yes. Him.

It was a cacophony of sound, I heard distant sirens approaching, but even surrounded by the fractured symphony of noise I heard Karen's breath escape, taking with it the petal pink of her lips. I waited for the next inhale, the color to return to her velvet lips then just the same pale yellow as her skin. I strained to hear her inhale. I prayed to hear. It never came.

The fire department was the first to arrive and they began to move people away. I still hadn't moved and wasn't about to. A fireman knelt next to Karen across from Mr. Svinth. The fireman lifted Karen's tiny wrist and delicate hand and felt for a pulse. After some time he stopped trying, but he continued to hold her soft hand.

I began to hear my name tossed about like dirty laundry in the wash. Whose gun is it? Jimmy's. Who shot her? Jimmy. Where is this Jimmy? Jimmy. Jimmy. I wished that my name were something other than Jimmy. And I wished I had brought my dad's medal, more than anything I wished I had brought the Purple Heart and that the cherry blossom pink could return to Karen's lips.

The echoes of my name brought with them the first police officer. He yanked me to my feet. The fireman gently placed his hand on Mr. Svinth's shoulder and as the policeman dragged me away I saw that Mr. Svinth was crying.

Hundreds of eyes followed me as the police officer hauled me away by my upper arm. He held my arm high and I was forced along on my tiptoes. I thought I was being taken to the principal's office, but the officer continued past the office and marched me out to the parking lot. There were two fire trucks and five police cars, lights still blinking and flashing like Christmas in the summer heat. An ambulance had arrived but I hadn't seen any medical technicians. Maybe I'd missed them in the crowd. Maybe they knew they were too late.

The entire time I was being dragged to the parking lot the police officer shot me with questions, never leaving time for an answer. Where'd you get the gun? Why did you bring it to school? Who taught you to shoot? Did you have a fight with that girl? Why did you do it? Why, you little sonofabitch?

I would have tried to answer if he had given me a chance, but he wasn't much in a giving mood and a chance never came. I couldn't see his full nametag, just the letters at the end. They spelled out 'man' like Truman or Foreman or Kingman. He put me in the back of a Dodge St. Regis patrol car. It was hot but there weren't any handles to roll down the windows. It was quiet like the moment between heartbeats.

Then Officer Something-man opened the door saying, "This is him." An older man appeared and squatted down on his haunches to talk to me. "I'm Detective Norwood," he said. He looked me over then said, "Show me your hands." I complied, turning them over so he could see both sides. He then stood up and said to the officer, "I'll take him. Drive mine back to the station." Detective Norwood closed the car door, handed his keys to the officer and climbed in the patrol car.

I couldn't see where we were going. Detective Norwood didn't turn on the siren. All he said as he drove was, "You okay back there?" I said, "Uh huh."

❋ ❋ ❋

I sat, my legs crossed at the ankle, in a chair next to Detective Norwood's desk. When he brought me to his desk, he had dragged the chair from opposite the desk and set the chair beside it. My blood-soaked pants had begun to dry and turn sticky as I sat there. I stared at my blood-covered hands. They never told me specifically that Karen was dead and that I'd killed her. Officer Something-man pointed me out to another policeman and I overheard him say, "That's the kid who shot and killed that little girl at the elementary school." I was then forever branded.

Detective Norwood seemed old and authoritarian dressed in a white shirt, red tie, blue blazer and gray Levi's Action Slacks™. Looking back on it he was probably younger than I am now.

I told Detective Norwood about the Purple Heart. About how I intended to bring it and had gone to the attic. I told him about cigar boxes and about how no one keeps cigars in them. I had committed the youngest school shooting in the nation's history and I'm sitting there talking about cigar boxes full of money and bolts and crayons. And I could hear myself saying it and it made me sick. It was as though I knew the gun was loaded and I was going to shoot it and kill her...I had always known. I wanted to throw up.

Two cops in suits had arrested Uncle Henry and brought him in for questioning. I could see his handcuffed wrists at a small table through the window of an interrogation room. I could only see his hands and sleeves but I knew it was Henry even though I never saw his face. I had already told Detective Norwood that Henry was sleeping when I crawled into the attic but that didn't seem to make any difference. Nothing I said would ever make any difference. The cartoons had lied; Karen was never going to be in the next scene.

Of course Uncle Henry had no idea that there was a loaded gun in the footlocker that once had gone through World War Two. He had no idea that I had crept into the attic while he slept. But they kept him there for hours.

From time to time some policemen would come, squat down in front of me and ask more questions and I would answer but it wouldn't change anything. I had made a choice; I did not bring the Purple Heart and would never bring it. And I sat in that chair and day drifted toward night.

And still I sat in the chair looking at the dried blood. I looked up to Detective Norwood.

"I need to use the restroom," I said.

Detective Norwood led me down a hallway toward the rest rooms. Through a window I saw Linda seated in a waiting area looking at us. She saw the blood covering my arms and hands. She stood as we passed.

In a restroom stall I bent over the toilet; my hands gripped the seat. I tried to vomit, but nothing happened. My stomach turned and squeezed but even it refused to provide the slightest relief. I exited the stall under the watchful gaze of the detective. I went to the sink and ran the hot water. I watched the steam rise.

They did not charge Henry and he was eventually released.

The world had grown dark by the time Detective Norwood escorted me through a door to the front desk area. Linda was there.

"Is my mother coming?" I said to her.

"No honey."

She turned and signed a document. We walked out of the police station and into the night. Henry was sitting in Linda's car waiting for us. He had aged ten years. He flashed me a small smile that let me know he didn't hate me.

I sat belted in the back seat as Linda drove Henry and me home. Henry stared out the passenger window. I could see his reflection looking out into the night sky. I believe he was being crushed under a cross, a cross that wasn't really his to bear. We never spoke about it. Not once. Not ever.

We pulled up to the house. I trailed Henry and Linda into the house. The house was quiet and dark; the only illumination came from a couple of lit candles resting on the mantel. Alex and Mary were sitting in the shadows. Alex gave a small nod in my direction.

I stood alone waiting for something, anything from my mother. She couldn't look at me. I had become my father's son.

My eyes dropped to the floor. I continued on into my room. I took off my blood-covered sneakers. I unbuttoned my torn "good" shirt and stripped off my blood-soaked pants. I padded in bare feet upstairs and ran bathwater. I soaked in Lady Macbeth's tub.

In bed, bearing all the weight of guilt since Cain, I stared stoically at the ceiling. And even though I knew I had scrubbed with Lava soap, even though I knew I had thrown my good clothes in the trash, I could still feel the sticky blood on my hands, the stiff pants against my legs, the ragged shirt against my chest. I still feel them.

In the dark I could see my dad's face staring at thick white paint on a prison bathroom wall. I could see Mary's beautiful defeated eyes looking at shadows. But when I closed my eyes I saw Karen, staring at me with wondering blue eyes and deathly pale lips. My lower lip quivered and I couldn't make it stop.

Epilogue

The funeral was two days later. They closed the school for the day. I did not attend the services. But later, after everyone had left...the casket was white and I thought of satin and velvet and lace. I watched from a tree, the same tree I sat in just one week earlier, as workers peeled back the Astroturf and filled the grave with dirt. It felt like it had been months--years since I had hung upside-down from that tree, not merely one week. It didn't take long for the workers to fill in the grave. That was wrong. It should have taken so much longer, maybe eighty years.

The district attorney had determined the shooting was an accident and I was not charged. But I was guilty all the same and justice was not served. I had snuffed out Karen's life and ground it in the dirt like a barely smoked Belair cigarette.

We moved within days and I never went back to that school. The school is no longer there, it's become a housing development and the scene of my crime is now under someone's garage.

Mary and I were constantly moving: house to house, welfare to work to welfare, school to school. My body grew, but some of me, part of me, most of me was blood-soaked and forever seven going on eight. I had gone to twelve different schools before I was graduated from high school. But it was always the same--the stain of what I had done preceded me wherever I went. I could have self-medicated, I could have marched lock step behind my dad, down the alcohol trail. Instead I tried to lose myself in books. John Webster, Albert Camus, F. Scott Fitzgerald didn't know me or what I had done.

Uncle Henry dropped off the grid, no phone, no address. He would show up from time to time, never announced, never planned, sometimes with short hair, sometimes long, always with two-weeks worth of beard. We'd drive up to the top of Sonoma Mountain when the sky was clear and you could see all the way to the bay. Or we'd drive into The City and take the cable car to Chinatown for Chinese food. Linda was no longer in his life. It was like she was there, had always been there, then she was gone.

When I was nine he paid me to help paint his house before he sold it; he talked about his brother Tommy. He and Tommy had painted their grandfather's house, white and Sagamore Green. Henry wanted to paint his the same but apparently Sherwin-Williams didn't have Sagamore Green any longer. I didn't know what color Sagamore Green was, still don't. Henry told me about painting the trim and lying on the roof and talking with Tommy about a bicycle, a Black Phantom. And for a few moments I would forget about cigar boxes and purple hearts.

Henry said that he thought that there was a direct correlation, a direct line, from the best day in your life to the worst. He didn't say that the day on the roof with Tommy was the best day, and he didn't say anything at all about his worst day. He did finish the thought, although that was many years later.

I left home the summer before my seventeenth birthday. Well, more accurately Mary decided to move once again and that time I decided not to follow. I got by sleeping on couches, in garages or storage sheds and tried as much as possible to leave the smallest ripple in the lives of people who offered their help. I survived.

Mom and I, we became a greeting card family, exchanging professionally written sentiments on appropriate Hallmark dates, often with forwarded addresses and occasionally returned as undeliverable, but always signed with "Love." In that I suspect we aren't much different from many sons and mothers; two lives diverged in the woods.... But then sometimes I'll smell cornbread, I'll smell cornbread and think of Henry and Alex, and Mary sitting on the sand in the tender glow of the setting sun.

It was there on that same sand twenty years after the start of the first day of third grade when Henry finished his thought about the best and worst day. I had driven to the coast on a clear cold September morning. Waves stroked the shore like a tender lover. I saw smoke from a campfire. It was Henry's fire. His two-weeks worth of beard had started to grey. He was heating a pot of coffee over a blazing teepee of driftwood. He didn't seem surprised to see me. He offered me a cup of coffee, which he poured into a plastic glass. It was hot and strong. We sat and sipped and listened to the waves.

I asked Henry where he was living, he said America. I asked how long he'd been there on the beach. He said it'd been a few days, but he didn't try to keep track of them. He asked if I remembered helping him paint his house. I told him I did, that he'd been thinking about best and worst days. He said he'd thought more about it. He said that after the worst day every breath thereafter was a promise, that by definition, this day had to be better than the worst day.

After some time, I rose and brushed sand from my jeans. I left him there, sitting on the beach, grey hair sprinkled randomly about his head like afterthoughts. I didn't tell him that for me, each day after was just a continuation of that worst day.

Through the years I was reminded with tragic regularity of what I had done. All too often on television I would hear a news reporter say, "The incident was the youngest school shooting since..." Since.

I never touched a gun again. If I had I would have blown my brains out a thousand times by now.

❋ ❋ ❋

So now in a small cemetery on the side of the hill, rows of headstones standing silent sentry I find myself once again at your grave. And I feel like I'm still wearing a stained and sticky ratty pair of Adidas sneakers, two sizes too large.

I read the news today.

I stare at the small marker that reads: Karen Brownsburger, August 18, 1973 - September 8, 1981. Cherished Forever. I am almost surprised by the shadow of a man that is cast near your grave. My shadow.

I read the news. A six-year-old Midwestern boy brought a gun to school and just like that a record that should have stood forever was broken.

What were his choices? Will he now live my life? And who am I now?

I didn't come to tell you that. I guess I was looking for some kind of forgiveness. But you can't forgive. And I, I can't forget. And all I'm left with is a handful of "I'm sorrys" that ring and die... just hollow echoes in empty canyons.

I place a small cherry blossom gently on the marker. The shadow of a man stands and walks away; the sound of boots on gravel marks the way.

I know a joke. Why did the elephant wear bloody red tennis shoes?

Say why.

THE END